42 Days for Murder

© 2013
Cover © Can Stock Photo/pepperbox
Layout by Bryce Pearson

Black Curtain Press
PO Box 632
Floyd VA 24091

ISBN 13: 978-1515426240

First Edition
10 9 8 7 6 5 4 3 2 1

42 Days for Murder

Roger Torrey

CHAPTER ONE

Lester came in my office with the sun hitting his glasses and making them shine like headlights. He said: "Joey Free and some other man are outside and want to see you."

He stopped, took off his glasses and started to polish them. He can't see two feet in front of his nose without them, but he peered over toward where I was and added:

"Joey is drunk, I think. I think the other man is drunk, too."

I said: "It's early in the day for that, even for Joey. But I wouldn't let it bother me."

Lester's tone showed it bothered him plenty. He had the notion Joey Free built the world and then a neat little picket fence around it. And Lester's only nineteen and doesn't appreciate the solid joy a drinking man takes with his drink.

Then Joey and his friend followed Lester in.

Joey is big and stocky, with a body like a keg. He was supposed to have a lot of money and to be spending it on women and liquor far too fast. It wasn't gossip because I'd been to parties at Joey's place. The man with him was tall and slat-like and looked very solemn and serious. I had to take another look before I could see the look was put on for effect; that the man was just carrying his liquor carefully.

Joey is ordinarily careful about his clothes. But he was dressed in clothes that looked as though they'd been thrown at him. The coat and trousers didn't match, he wore no necktie, and his shirt was filthy dirty.

The other man looked no better; he couldn't well have looked worse.

Joey gave me his big toothy grin and said: "Hi, Shean! I brought you a customer. We just got in. This is Tod Wendel. Toddy, tell the man your troubles."

I said I was glad to meet Mr. Wendel and Lester put his glasses back on and scurried around and got chairs. I introduced him to Wendel, saw the doubtful look Wendel gave him, and let Lester do the explaining, which he always does. Lester said:

"My great-uncle left me some money so I bought an interest in Mr. Connell's agency. I've always been interested in criminology. It's a fascinating subject."

Lester's a lanky kid who looks sixteen and no older. I could see Wendel's estimation of the Connell agency take a drop but Joey helped things out with:

"Shean got himself a partner and five grand along with him. Shean will do anything for money and admits it."

I said: "Where in hell did you get the rig? You look like a bum, Joey."

"In Reno," he said. "That's what Toddy wants to talk to you about. Toddy and I went to Yale together. I met him in Reno when he wired me."

I said to Lester: "Ask Miss Gahagan to come in and make notes, kid," and to Wendel:

"Suppose you tell me about it."

Wendel told his story and it didn't seem to make much sense. According to him, he was in the money; most of it in two little steamships and a South American importing business. He'd married a girl named Ruth Carstairs three years before and they'd never had a cross word between them. He swore to that, with tears in his eyes. He'd gone to South America two months before, and just returned to New York.

And then he went home and found mama gone. Without a word or note left for him. Just a vacant apartment and empty closet space where her clothes had been.

He admitted he went a little goofy then. But he got himself together, found the apartment house manager, and discovered his wife and her maid had left for Reno, with the express purpose of divorcing him.

So he followed them to Reno.

Here Joey Free took up the tale. He said: "The first I knew about it was when I got a wire from Toddy. It just said 'Meet me Golden Eagle Reno at once.' Naturally I joined him there."

"I probably wouldn't have wired Joey," Wendel told me, "except that Joey was in New York just before I left for South America and we saw a bit of each other. I remembered he lived here and I thought he might be able to help me."

I said: "I don't get the idea of you needing help. You must have walked on your wife's pet corn some way you don't remember. Why in hell don't you talk to her and get it straightened out?"

Wendel looked as though he was going to break down and sob. He said, with tears in his voice: "That's just it. She won't talk with me. I tried to see her and she had me thrown out of the house. It was then I wired Joey; I was desperate."

"And then what happened?"

Joey grinned and said: "We both got thrown out. And boy, what I mean we got thrown out. I've been heaved out of a lot of places during my sinful life but they did a masterful job. See!"

He pointed to his eye and I could see where it had been blacked. I hadn't noticed this before because his face was so dirty. He went on with: "I argued with two of the tough babies she's got guarding her and that was the wrong thing to do. They weren't fooling. I thought I got a couple of broken ribs out of it, too, but they were just bruises."

Wendel took up the tale of woe with: "And then we went to the police. I'd already been there but they'd said there was nothing they could do about it. That I had no right to talk with my own wife unless she was willing. But Joey knew a man who knew some of the police and we told him about it."

"And got exactly nowhere," Joey Free put in. "Ruth's living at her lawyer's house and the cops don't want any part of him. He's some big shot named Crandall; a pretty smart egg, I hear. So there was nothing else to do but go on a bat. Toddy was pretty low and my shiner and the bruises I've got to nigger with gave me an excuse. We put on a pip, Shean."

"How come the tramp makeup?"

Joey had the grace to blush, which is something I never expected to see. "It was like this. We'd drink for a while and then buck the games for excitement. Someway we got to hell and gone out on Virginia Street and some thug held us up. And the dirty———..." He looked at Miss Gahagan, who was taking this all down in shorthand and said: "Excuse me!"

She said: "I've heard worse than that in this office," and grinned at him.

He grinned back at her and said: "I bet you never heard a worse thing than happened to us. He made us take off our pants, so we couldn't chase him. He took the pants, every damned bit of identification we had, what money the games had left us, and ran away. We were in a hell of a fix."

Lester said, from the side: "I understand that taking the victim's trousers to prevent pursuit is fairly common practice among hold-up men. It must be very embarrassing."

Both Joey Free and Wendel said that this was an understatement. Both the Gahagan wench and I were laughing. I said: "And what then?"

"We went to the police station again," Joey said. "Of course we were both drunk and we didn't have any pants on. We got within a block of the place, hiding and ducking around to keep from being seen, but some damn fool woman saw us and called the police and said two maniacs with no clothes were running around her front yard. The police came, four of them, and they threw us in jail for the rest of the night. The next morning we left."

I said: "It seems odd to me, Mr. Wendel, that you'd give up your attempt at seeing your wife so easily. After making the trip out from New York and all."

"We didn't have any choice," he told me. "We were practically forced to leave. That's what I want you to do; go up there and investigate this for me and find out what's the matter with Ruth.."

"Why didn't you talk with Crandall about it? That's the name of your wife's lawyer, isn't it?"

"Well, Joey did. I think that was the reason we were forced to leave. Crandall seems to have a lot of influence there."

I wasn't understanding this talk about being forced to leave and I said so. And they'd left the pants story unfinished and I wanted to know about that. So Joey said:

"Oh the cops gave us some pants. They took up a collection. We were on a plane for here a half hour after leaving the jail."

"Why the rush?"

Joey lost his grin, for the first time since he'd been there. He said, slowly and solemnly: "Well, it was a forced put. A big guy with a mean look and a gun put us on board, gave us tickets, and told us not to come back. He acted as though he meant what he said."

"Why in God's name didn't you tell this to the cops there? There's always one around an airport."

Wendel said: "That was just it. It was a cop that put us on board. I told you that man Crandall has influence."

CHAPTER TWO

I told Wendel I'd look into the thing for him and they left for Joey Free's apartment. They wanted a drink and needed one; they'd headed for my office directly from the airport. They wanted clothes, and needed them as badly as the drink. But before they left, I took Joey to one side and said:

"I'll do a little checking on the Nevada law today and see if I can work out an angle on this. But I'd like to talk it over with you, personally, before I leave."

"Sure," he said. Come up tonight. I'll probably be having a little celebration for old Toddy, but we can find a corner that'll be quiet enough to talk in."

"It sounds dopy to me," I told him. "A guy's wife don't usually start out after a divorce without saying anything. Usually she's said so damned much he's glad to see her leave."

Joey nodded toward Lester. "Going to take the kid along?"

"Sure! That's what he paid his five grand in for, to be a detective. I've got to give him his money's worth, don't I?"

He nodded toward the Gahagan wench. She's red-headed, Irish, and an eyeful. He said: "When you come up, why not bring the gal? She'd appreciate it and *I'd* appreciate it."

"To hell with you. I've seen your parties. She'd black-mail around the office here and I couldn't get her to do a thing. I have a hard enough time with her now, without making a pet of her."

"I'd make a pet of her."

"You dope! You would. About eight, I'll be there."

"Fine, Shean!"

Everybody shook hands and, when they'd gone, Lester said: "I can see, Shean, that this is going to be a very odd case. Something that will tax your ability to the utmost."

The Gahagan said: "Nuts! All Shean has to do is look around and find the gal's new boy friend. She wouldn't leave her old man without a reason and that'll be it."

Lester looked wise and said: "Ah, yes! The sex motive that is back of so many crimes."

"What d'ya mean crime?" I asked him. "Is it any crime for a gal to get tired of her old man and want to trade him in on a new model?"

He argued: "There's something funny about this, just the same. Or why would the police put Joey Free and Mr. Wendel on the plane, bodily. That's suspicious, Shean."

I thought the same but didn't admit it.

The party was going nicely at eight o'clock. I could hear it through the door, and I had no doubt about Joey's neighbors hearing it through the walls. I rang the bell, and a little blonde opened the door and said: "Oh, it's tall and dark and handsome. Come in, mister tall and dark and handsome."

She was holding a highball glass and she'd held too many of them. I could see she wasn't going to last the party out. I went in, saw Wendel sitting in a corner and looking gloomy, and Joey Free with about eight assorted women around him. There were also half a dozen men, but Joey was on the inside track. Joey saw me and called:

"Hi, Shean! You're just in time."

I asked just in time for what and he said he was referring to a drink. I got him and the drink to one side and said:

"Now look, Joey! This is a dopy set-up. Don't take it wrong, but has this guy got the money to pay me if I go on it?"

"He's got plenty," Joey said. "When his father died, the inheritance tax was between two and three hundred thousand. He was the only child. Figure it out."

"Because it's going to cost plenty. I'm going to have to put out some money around that town and not put it on a report blank and expense account."

"Why not? Why can't you put it down?"

"When you're bribing cops you don't keep a record. Not unless you're a chump."

He said slowly: "I wouldn't say you're exactly a chump, Shean. But there's this. That gal had more than an excuse to leave old Toddy. This is the first time he's busted loose since he was married. It was all work and no play for him and it's a little discouraging for a girl to have to listen about so and so taking up his option and whether such and such will stand by his lease or not. Toddy's a good egg, but he's business through and through. It's my idea that the gal just got fed up with him."

"What does she look like?"

He went someplace and came back with a picture of a good-looking dark girl. He said: "I got this when I went East, just before Toddy made the South American trip. Keep it, if you like."

I said: "I like."

The blonde girl came over and acted as though she wanted to sit in my lap. Only I was standing up and didn't have one, I fended her away and Joey tried to get something on the radio they could dance to, but didn't do so well. He came back in a minute, which gave me a break with the blonde, and said:

"Hey, Shean! Some of this mob want to dance, or what is supposed to pass for it. Stick around and play a little piano for us, hey?"

"I've quit that business," I told him. "I haven't played a job for two years and more. There's no money in it, and that's all I'll work for."

He pointed over to the piano and said: "The hell there isn't. There's a hundred dollars in it, if you'll stick it out until the neighbors and the manager make you stop."

I said: "Just make the check out to Shean Connell," and headed for the piano.

The manager didn't threaten to call the police until after three. But after all, a hundred dollars is a lot of money, even if you say it slow and easy. And I'd been in Reno before and know I could never pad up an expense account enough to break even there; there's too many ways of spending money in the place.

CHAPTER THREE

Lester and I drove up from the city and we didn't get in town until after five. So we checked in at the Golden Eagle and got cleaned up and fed before anything else. Then I said to Lester:

"Okey, kid. You stay here and hold the fort and I'll go and talk with the Chief."

Lester said: "Can't I go with you?"

"Stay here and read a good book. I don't know this Chief, except by reputation."

Lester put on his criminologist look. "Are you sure it's a wise step, Shean? After all, the police forced Joey and Mr. Wendel aboard the plane. It's very possible they will be antagonistic toward us and our mission."

I said: "Now look! They may be. But an outside cop has to co-operate with the law every time. They're not only antagonistic but rabid if you don't. Do you understand?"

"In my opinion, it would be wiser to look the situation over first."

I wanted to laugh but I tried to look stern instead. "Now, Lester, we agreed I was to decide anything that came up and that my decision would be final. Isn't that right?"

He said it was. I said: "All right, then. I've decided to talk with Chief Kirby, before doing anything else. Now that's final. Understand?"

He said he did, and looked very sad while he said it. All the matter with him was that he wanted to go along with me; didn't want to miss anything. But I couldn't see walking into the Chief of Police's office with Lester in tow; Wendel and Joey Free had already put me under a handicap by whatever fool stunt they'd done to get themselves chased out of town. I blamed them for that, knowing Joey Free and some of the dizzy stunts he'd pulled in the city. And I knew of Chief Kirby by reputation. He was supposed to be a damn good man and he had a tough job to hold with Reno as open as it was. Lester would have been no help.

Chief of Police Kirby was a medium-sized, medium-aged man. No particular coloring or feature that stood out at all. And very quiet. He listened, while I told him all that Wendel and Joey Free had told me and then said:

"You understand, of course, that Mr. Wendel had no legal right to see his wife if she objected? You've got that point straight, haven't you?"

I said I realized that, but that Wendel seemed sincerely in love with his wife and only wanted to talk with her and find out what he'd done to cause her action. Kirby didn't answer this but just stood up and said:

"Come on and take a ride with me."

We climbed in a police car and he drove to where a sign said: HILLARD MORTUARY. Kirby explained:

"We use this; the city hasn't modern conveniences," and I had a notion of what he was going to show me.

But not who.

A short, smiling little man met us, acting as though we were doing him a favor by calling, and the three of us went in a side room.

The girl was there. The woman, rather. She had been around thirty apparently—fair-looking, too, except that her nose was too big and beaked. Black hair and rather dark-skinned. There was a blue puckered slit a bit to the side in her neck, and Kirby pointed this out to me and said:

"Knife wound. Hit the big artery."

I said: "Nasty thing, a shiv is. Who is she?"

He said, as though reading from a police report: "Francine Debreaux. French nationality. In this country four years and her passport and papers in order. Mrs. Todhunter Wendel's personal maid for the last year. Had fair references. New York is checking these for me now."

"Where'd you find her? Where'd she get the shiv in her neck?"

The undertaker, who it seemed was also the local Coroner, said: "She was in an alley, back of the MIDNIGHT CLUB. The knife wound didn't kill her at once; she probably took two or three minutes to bleed out."

Kirby said: "Whoever did it held something over her mouth. Her lips are slightly bruised, if you'll notice. There was a cook and dishwasher in the club, within fifteen feet of where this happened, and they never heard a sound."

"Did you check on them?"

He looked at me as though this was a silly question, which it was. He said he'd checked them, naturally, and that neither had known the woman as far as he could tell. Without anything more he turned away and toward the door and I followed him, with the undertaker bringing up the rear. The undertaker followed us out to the car, shook hands with me and said he hoped to see me again, though under pleasanter circumstances of course, and Kirby drove away, heading back toward the police station.

He didn't say a word during the trip back, but after he'd led the way into his office he said: "Now what d'ya know that'll help on this? We've got an open town here but murder's fairly rare. I want to keep it so."

I said: "I've told you everything I know. What did Mrs. Wendel have to say about this? When did it happen?"

"Between eleven and eleven-thirty last night. Mrs. Wendel doesn't seem to know of a reason for it, nor does Mr. Crandall, her lawyer. What are you holding out on me? What's all this about, Connell?"

I told him I didn't have the faintest idea. That all I knew about the thing was what I'd told him. He listened to me, very quietly, but he had a veil over his eyes and I couldn't tell whether he believed me or not. Apparently he didn't, because he said:

"Now listen! This is my town and I run it my way. Get it? We're open here because that's the way the city dads want it. People come here with money to spend and we let them spend it the way they want. But we keep an eye out for them right along with it. They're entitled to that for their ante. We can't keep 'em from making damn fools of themselves but we can keep most of the wolves off their backs. Does this mean anything to you?"

I said it was a very nice speech, only I didn't phrase it just that way. He got the idea, though. He reddened a bit around the cheek-bones but he didn't raise his voice. Which showed nice control. "I mean just this, Connell! I've got no objection to your coming in here and doing a job of work. I don't hold any briefs for your kind of work, but you're entitled to make a living the way you want. But that's all. No rough stuff; none of the trick stuff you can pull in the city and get away with."

"I don't understand, Chief," I said.

"You understand all right. No cutting corners and no throwing curves. This woman lives here; you don't. If she wants to talk to you it's fine with me. If she doesn't, let her alone. You're butting in on her business and I want you to remember it. When did you say you got here?"

I knew what he was thinking about and said: "At eleven o'clock last night I was playing piano for a private party and working like hell at it. At Joey Free's apartment; you can call him and check this."

And then I threw the harpoon; not hard but enough to get under his hide. I kept my face straight and added:

"You ought to remember Joey Free, Chief. He's one of the two you bum-rushed out of here. You know the other, Wendel, the guy I'm supposed to be working for."

His cheeks got a bit redder. "Listen, Connell. I didn't think you had anything to do with that alley killing last night. Get that out of your head."

I grinned and said I'd rather got the idea he didn't like private cops and didn't put anything past them, up to and including alley murders. I made a joke out of it and meant it; I really liked the man. He took it the way it was meant and smiled back and said:

"I meant that the right way, Connell, and you know it. After all, I just work here. The local boys can put pressure on me, if you know what I mean."

He meant Crandall, the Wendel woman's lawyer, but I didn't say I knew this. I just said that a cop worked for the city, of course, and was responsible to a lot of people. In fact, all the tax-payers.

He said that was the theory... and grinned as though it was funny, which it was. There were probably a dozen men in town who could crack the whip and make him jump and he cracked the whip for the rest of the town. Small towns as open as that one are like that, always.

We shook hands and he asked where I was staying. I told him, then said:

"I'm here, but not for long. Too much money for my kind of job. The people I'll meet will think I'm going high-hat."

"That's where Free and Wendel stayed." He started to laugh. "That Free's a kick. In any other town but this one, he'd have been lynched."

"What did he do?"

"Well, he and Wendel were both drunk, as I get the story. They went up to their room and Wendel passed out. But Free had noticed some blonde gal in a room two doors away and he got hot for her. So he climbed out his window, hung onto the building in some way that I'm damned if I can figure, and did a human fly act around to the blonde's room."

"That sounds like Joey. He's wacky, when he's stiff."

"Well, the blonde was going to bed and was dressed for it. Rather, she wasn't dressed for it. She looked up and saw this Free grinning at her through the window and she went nuts. She thought he was a burglar, I guess. She ran out in the hall and raised hell about it and the house cop went up and found Joey sitting on her bed and waiting for her to come back and play. I didn't hear about it until the next day. It didn't make difference; I wouldn't have done anything about it unless the blonde had signed a complaint, anyway."

I asked whether the blonde had any clothes on when she ran out in the hall and he said he'd heard not. I said I could see I was going to like the town; that the nudist idea had always fascinated me. Kirby grinned and said:

"That's the pay-off. Free didn't have to do a monkey trick along the wall to get in that room. Hell! All he'd have had to do would have been to knock on the door. She'd have let him in. Probably dragged him in."

"That didn't have anything to do with you chasing him out of town, did it?"

Kirby started drawing rings on a desk blotter and broke the pencil point doing it. Then he stared out the window and said:

"Sure is a swell day. You've got to admit we've got climate here."

I agreed with him and he stood up and we shook hands. I told him I'd tell him when I got a new address and he followed me to the door of his office. Then he said, very softly:

"You're bucking against quite a man here, mister. I suppose you know that."

I said I'd gathered that. And then: "D'ya think the maid getting killed in that alley has anything to do with Mrs. Wendel's business? Can you see a connection, Chief?"

"I'll know more about it when I get New York's check on those references of hers. It's got me puzzled and I don't like puzzles. Not when there's knife murders mixed in them, anyway."

I said I didn't blame him, thanked him, and started to leave. He called after me:

"I'll be seeing you, Connell."

CHAPTER FOUR

I left the station and stopped in the first bar on my route. It was called the RUSTIC and the decoration scheme wasn't too original. Pine logs with the bark on them covered the walls and the bar itself was a big tree cut in half and polished. Big sugar-pine cones were festooned all over the place with deer heads and guns on the walls. The place even smelled piny and out-doorsy.

By the time I'd taken my first drink all the way down I'd figured the place was phony. The logs on the wall were just slabs from some sawmill; the bar was geed up in the same way and the pine cones looked as though they'd been dipped in shellac. The guns looked as though they'd come from an Army and Navy auction and the deer were Michigan White-tailed deer instead of the mule deer native around there.

The smell came from pine incense being burned in saucers back of the bar.

I was looking this all over and wondering if anybody could get the real western feeling from a spot like that, when somebody came up from behind me and smacked me on the back and said:

"Shean Connell! Jeese! Shean Connell!"

The wallop on the back had been hard and there was a second in which I thought I'd maybe cough up my drink. It stuck, though. I turned around and Kewpie Martin reached for my hand and began pumping it up and down and saying:

"Shean Connell! Well I'll be damned!"

This over and over again.

I'd worked with Kewpie on a roadhouse job four years before that. He was supposed to be a saxophone player and singer as well as being able to Master of Ceremonies a bit. It was all a lie. He had a soggy tone on sax beside having no technic; he sang flat and through his nose, and his M. C. stuff wasn't funny. Just pitiful.

He got by because he was such a swell guy to work with. Everybody would hold him up on the job just to keep him there. He was about five-six but he weighed two-fifty, at the least. He wasn't quite bald but had a little tuft of hair like Kewpie dolls have. Which is why the name, I suppose. I said: "Well, Christ, it's Kewpie. Where've you been, kid?"

"Around and around. Like the music. How long you been

here?"

"Just got here."

"Looking for a spot?"

I said I was looking for a drink, more than anything else, at least at that time. I bought and Kewpie bought and then he said: "You could land here, if you want. I hear they're looking for a man, now."

I'd spotted a piano over in the corner of the room before that. It was prettied up the same way; had itself decorated in the pine motif. I nodded at it and said:

"Nuts! Me play a box like that? That'll be the day."

He said: "You always was a fussy bastard, Shean."

I agreed and said: "I don't even like their whisky. Let's go down to my place."

He asked me where I was staying and I told him the Golden Eagle. He smiled admiringly and said that I always was one for putting on the Ritz. We started out the door and met Kirby, face to face, and Kirby said:

"Hi! Have a drink, Connell."

If I'd stayed, I'd have had to introduce Kewpie and I was afraid Kirby might crack about why I was in town. It might do no harm, but I hadn't decided just what I was going to do or how I was going to try and do it and I couldn't see any reason for letting Kewpie in on secrets. So I said to Kirby:

"Thanks, Chief! Some other time. I'm late for a date now."

Kirby said "Too bad!" and strolled over to the bar, and Kewpie and I went out and down the street. Kewpie said: "Jeese! Just in town and know the Chief already. Are you hot, keed?"

I said I wasn't and that I'd known Kirby for a long time.

We kept on to the hotel.

Lester was in the room, which I was afraid he'd be. Kewpie and I came in and I said "Lester, I want you to meet an old friend of mine. Kewpie Martin. Kewpie's an entertainer. Kewpie, this is Lester Hoyt."

They shook hands and I winked at Lester over Kewpie's shoulder. Lester missed it entirely, Kewpie said to him:

"Hi, Lester. You in the music business, too?"

Lester looked puzzled and said he wasn't. I sidled over closer to him, having an idea what was coming.

It came. Lester quit goggling at Kewpie, who was really something to look at, if you like chubby fat men, and said to me "Did you see the..."

I got him on the instep with my heel when he'd gotten that much out. He yelped, lifted his foot and held it with both hands, glared at me and said: "Gee, Shean, that hurt."

"I must have stumbled," I said, and winked at him again. It still was a miss. He sat down on the edge of the bed, still holding his foot, and this time he managed to say it. Just: "Did you see the Chief, Shean?"

"Sure," I said, and put my finger up to my face. And then to Kewpie: "I was telling Lester that I used to know the Chief. We weren't exactly pals, or anything like that, but I knew him. Maybe I told you about it, Kewpie?"

Kewpie looked from Lester to me. And then looked puzzled. The little fat devil was no fool and smelled something sour. I got on the phone and ordered soda and cracked ice, just to change the subject, and when it came, mixed two highballs. Kewpie looked inquiringly at Lester and Lester said: "I never drink."

This as though he was proud of it. Kewpie snorted, took half his highball down, and said: "Well, man and boy, I've been drinking for thirty-five years. Well, anyway thirty years, if you want to make me out a liar for a matter of five years or so. I haven't lost any weight from it."

Lester said, very seriously, that he could see this. Kewpie kept staring at him, as though trying to figure out whether the joke was on himself or Lester. Finally he said to me:

"Look, Shean! The C. C. C. wants a piano player. I'm thinking of moving to that spot myself. I got a bid last week. What d'ya say we talk to them and work together again?"

"What d'ya mean C. C. C.? Is it one of these government things?"

"Dope! That's the City and Country Club. It's new and it's getting a play. We can get a guaranty but the cat will run over it easy. What d'ya say?"

Lester showed signs of breaking out in speech and I shook my head at him and said to Kewpie: "Let's go out and look at it. What kind of a play does it get?"

"The big shots. The gals and guys with folding dough. They've got six weeks to spend here and they get tired of the same places. A new place will sometimes go bang for a while. I'll tell you now, Shean, the spot ain't so hot."

He turned to Lester and explained: "Shean's a fussy sort of bastard. He won't work in a joint. Or at least he didn't used to."

Lester had finally judged the angle. Of course he knew I was an ex-pianist. He said: "Do you want me to go along, Shean?"

Kewpie said hurriedly: "You'd better wait for him, kid," and I told Lester the same. We got outside and Kewpie said:

"Jeese, what a jerk! How come you got him on you, Shean? You always used to be lugging some tart around; now you're going for the boys. How come?"

I said: "Nuts! I just felt sorry for the kid. I picked him up on the highway. He was hitch-hiking and I brought him in with me. I didn't want the poor devil to starve. I'm softhearted, Kewpie."

He looked at me and said: "Okey, keed! I get it! I get it!"

"Get what?"

"The idea," he said slowly. "I don't know what the score is and I don't want to know. But don't give me that softhearted stall. You've got some reason for having the kid along and we both know it. It's not by business; I haven't got nose trouble."

"You're nuts, Kewpie."

"Maybe so. Any time Shean Connell gets good-hearted I'm nuts. I'll admit it."

CHAPTER FIVE

Kewpie hadn't been guilty of any understatement when he'd said the Three C Club wasn't so hot. It was about two miles from town, just a big, long barn-like affair sitting by the road. No shade around it. It was painted a bright and nasty red and the front of it was fixed so that it could be opened during hot weather. It was open then. There were a dozen cars parked in front of it and the gravel, in front of the place, was all chewed up in a way to show traffic there was heavy.

I parked my coupe and we went in.

The bar was at least forty feet long and there were three bar men behind it. All busy. There were at least fifty people in the place and lined up along the bar and it was only about seven-thirty. Far too early for any crowd as yet.

The bar itself was a classic, that is the bar and back bar combined. Whoever bought it in the first place must have done so well before the San Francisco fire. One of the old-fashioned, tremendously heavy and ornate things they used to go for. The back bar was stacked almost to the ceiling with glasses except for the space directly in front of the mirrors, and these were all soaped up with signs.

The bartenders didn't fit the bar. You'd expect to see old-time bar men back of a layout like that. The droopy-mustached, pomaded hair type. Big-paunched and all that goes with it. But the three back of the plank looked as though they'd been picked for a beauty contest. As though Hollywood had missed a bet on all three. Kewpie saw me staring at them and giggled and said:

"The bird that runs this is a smart son of a bitch. This place gets a big play from society women and he knows what they want. They've got a service bar for the back room, besides this."

He led me through a partition and into the back room. A dance floor about twenty feet square, a big Steinway grand at the side of it, and the whole thing lined with booths. The booths had curtains.

I went over to the piano, tried it with one hand, and a short dark man that looked Italian, came from one of the booths and said to me:: "You play?"

He saw Kewpie, looked at him as though he didn't want to,

and added: "Hi, Kewpie boy."

Kewpie beamed and said: "Hi, Gino. Can this guy play? He's tops. I worked with him at the Del Mar, in Tia Juana. Four years ago. He's really tops. This is Shean Connell."

The short man said eagerly: "Do you want a job? I'm looking for a piano player. To start tonight."

"'I just got in town," I said, "and I'm tired. I want to look around a bit before I get myself a spot."

"You'll do better here than any place in town. I'm telling you. Ain't that right, Kewpie?"

Kewpie said that was right and that he'd been telling me the same thing. I said, that if the job was as good as all that it seemed funny nobody was on it. The short man started to jump up and down and wring his hands. He almost moaned:

"These piano players they are pimps. I get one and what happens? What? I ask you? What happens?"

I said I didn't know.

"They get mixed up with women; that's what happens. Every time. If I keep one a week, I'm lucky. The women give them money and they're lazy and won't work unless they're broke and hungry. All piano players are the same."

Kewpie started to laugh and I wanted to. Gino said then: "But not you. I don't mean that. I can see you're not that kind."

Kewpie said: "Hell, Shean, take a few drinks and maybe you'll feel like working. You can knock off a few bucks for yourself tonight as well as not."

"I take it you're the boss?" I asked the short man. He said he was, that his name was Gino Rucci. I said: "Okey! I'll eat and take a few drinks and if I'm not too tired I'll work. How's that?"

"Mister, that will be fine. You understand. I'm stuck for a piano player."

I said: "Sure, I catch. But listen. About this woman business."

"Yes?"

I winked at Kewpie and said: "You might as well know, I won't work unless I've got women around me. I'm the type that has to have women around. Can you get 'em for me?"

"Sure! Sure! Sure, mister."

I said: "And you just getting through telling me that piano players were the pimps. Shame on you."

Kewpie and I turned and headed back for the bar. I looked back, as we went through the door, and Gino Rucci was standing by the piano and staring after us.

He was scratching his head and showing a lot of gold teeth in a grin and I figured my crack was probably more truth than poetry.

We had drinks and dinner—on the house. Rucci himself came back to us and asked if everything was okey. Then I ambled over to the piano and started noodling around, getting the feel of it. It was good, and in tune. Kewpie showed signs of wanting to sing and I didn't want that so early in the evening, so I said:

"Listen, kid! Call up the hotel and get the kid. Tell him to go out and get himself something to eat, if he hasn't already done it. Tell him that if he wants to, he can come out. Tell him to take a cab."

Kewpie said, very quickly: "I though he was broke and hitchhiking?"

I said, just as quickly: "And I thought you didn't have nose trouble?"

He grinned and went looking for a phone booth. He came back in a couple of minutes, said: "He wasn't in. He'd left no message because I asked for one."

I said he was probably out getting himself some dinner and just happened to turn my head toward the door.

In came Lester. He had his glasses on and they hid his eyes, but I'm willing to bet he was wild-eyed behind them. He looked proud and scared, all at the same time. He was with a big blonde wench that out-weighted him by at least forty pounds. She had on more than just a paint job. She was practically enameled. She had curves in the right places but she curved too much. And she was wearing a slinky, sneaky evening gown that brought the curves out to perfection. Far too much so. I thought of all the honky-tonks I'd worked and all the madames I'd known and couldn't think of a one that could hold a candle to this one. She out-madamed them all.

Lester saw me, waved a hand, very weakly, and she took him in tow and headed for a booth. I jerked my head at him and he stopped her and they had an argument for a moment. Lester won out. She went in the booth and he came over to the piano.

I said: "Where in Christ's name did you pick up the ut-slay? Or is it the other way around?"

He blushed and said feebly: "Now, Shean, you shouldn't talk like that."

"Why not?"

"She's a very nice lady."

"For my dough, she's a bum. I'll admit she's a *big* bum, though."

"She's a very nice lady," he argued again.

"Who is she?"

"Her name is Mrs. Heber. Well, there's more to it than that. It's really Mrs. Hazel George-Wolff-Heber. She's a ... a divorcee, I guess."

I said: "What d'ya mean guess? You know damn well."

He admitted he knew damn well.

"Where'd you meet her?"

"Well, I was in the lobby. Sitting there and waiting for you to come back. She was sitting by me. She got up and left her purse and I returned it to her. That's all. We just sort of ... well, sort of got talking and she wanted to come out here."

"You're no help to me, kid. You're supposed to be a hitchhiker I picked up. That's what I told Kewpie, anyway."

He got on the defensive and said: "I don't see why you told him that."

"I had reasons. Now listen. From now on your story is you're a college kid on a lark. You started hitch-hiking to Reno, just because your room-mate told you you didn't have the nerve. I'll tell Kewpie the same thing. Does this big tart know you've got any money?"

"Well ... I ... ugh..."

I said: "You put on a flash, hunh? Showed the bankroll That it?"

"Well, we had a couple of drinks before I left town. She... ugh... may have that idea."

"Does she know you're supposed to be a detective?"

"Of course not, Shean!" He sounded indignant on this. "I know enough to keep my mouth shut."

I said: "There's two sides to that argument. Yours and mine. Okey. Go on back to her. Tell her that I'm the guy that rode you in here. Let it go at that."

"Are you working here?"

I grinned and said: "Anyway for tonight. I want to see something."

"What?"

"The kind of women Gino Rucci can dig up."

He looked at me as though I was crazy. I quit riding him and said: "It's this way, kid. I've got to get close to the Wendel woman in some way. The Chief told me not to try and talk to her."

Lester looked indignant and said: "He can't do that. This is a free country; you've got a right to talk to somebody, certainly."

I said: "Okey, kid, you're right and the world's wrong. Remember this is Reno. Remember this Chief should know what he's talking about."

"What did he say, Shean?"

"He didn't come right out with it but he just the same as said what I told you. Now run along; I'm supposed to be working."

He went back to his booth and blonde.

CHAPTER SIX

About half an hour later I was just stalling around, on what I could remember of the SARI waltzes. There was nobody dancing; only about a dozen couples in the booths, though the bar was packed and noisy. Lester came over and grinned at me and said:

"Shean, will you play something we can dance to?"

I said: "Sure, if you hit the kitty. And don't put in two hits Go first class with a buck."

He looked pained and split the difference with a half dollar and I started out with a slow fox-trot. Kewpie came over and started to bellow out the chorus, and I couldn't decide whether that or his saxophone playing was worse.

I knew he'd do both, too enthusiastically, through the evening, and that I'd have a chance to decide. Lester and his blonde and two other couples started to cavort around and when Kewpie got through with his chorus he decided he'd take his sax out of wraps. He started to unpack it and I started to go to town on the tune.

It was an old-timer. *BREEZE.* The one that blew the gal away, according to the lyrics. An old Goodwin and Hanley number. A honey to go to town on. I got hot on it; it was always a pet of mine, and I could see two good-sized parties leave the bar and head for the back room and dance floor. Some of them started to dance and some went in the booths and I put in a few more licks for good measure and quit just in time because Kewpie had the mouthpiece on his sax and was showing signs of joining in, dry reed and all.

Lester came over right then. He took off his glasses and started polishing them and his eyes looked as big as saucers. He hissed at me:

"One of them's the Wendel woman! Hazel told me!"

I looked over at Kewpie, who was mouthing his sax reed and looking interested. Lester got the idea and said loudly: "That was fine, Shean! D'ya know *WHERE OR WHEN?*"

"That's a show tune. I don't know whether this place has got a license to play that sort of stuff." I looked at the kitty and then at Kewpie. And then winked.

Lester was getting smart. He bounced another fifty cent piece in the cat and Kewpie said: "That's working, Shean, old kid. That's the stuff to give the troops. If they think we're working here because we like music they're nuts. What key you taking it in?"

I said: "E flat, and if you play flat on that damned thing I'll take it away from you and shove it down your neck."

He said happily: "The same old Shean!" and we started out.

Things got going good by eleven o'clock. I'd spotted the Wendel woman by then and the crowd she was with and had been paying more attention to them than I had to the music —though this didn't seem to make any difference to anybody. Rucci had brought over at least ten assorted women and all of them had gushed over the music and said it must be wonderful to be able to play like that. The old line. Assorted women is right; blondes, brunettes, and one red head. All of them the same general type, however. Looking for excitement and all drinking too much by far.

The Wendel party was the exception, apparently they were nursing their drinks. There were six in the bunch, altogether; and my boss, Rucci, and a startlingly blonde gal he seemed to favor sat with them the bulk of the time.

The Wendel girl was prettier than I'd thought she'd be from her picture. Medium-sized, quite dark, and apparently not too fond of talking. At least she seemed to spend most of her time either listening or dancing.

There was a big bald-headed man that I thought might well be her lawyer, Crandall. Very boisterous in manner but the kind of manner that doesn't mean a thing. All on the surface. He had light blue eyes that didn't look merry at any time. Just smart and cagy. A tough baby, I figured.

There were two men that might have been twins, though they didn't look at all alike. The same type, exactly. My guess was private cops and that they were the guards Wendel and Joey Free had mentioned.

They had two girls with them and the less said about the girls the better. They both looked as if they should have been working for Lester's big blonde divorcee mama. That is, if the big tramp was running the kind of place that she looked as though she should be running.

It bothered me, this last. I couldn't figure why nice people like this Wendel girl would be out with such trash. And apparently friendly with Rucci and his girl friend.

But I kept on playing, sitting sidewise on the bench so I could watch the dancers, and pretty soon I decided I had the answer. The whole crowd was the same; just a mixture. You'd see girls that had lady written all over them dancing with men that had hustler written as —plainly.

And the opposite. Decent-looking men playing around with tramps.

I just put it down to Reno and let it go.

Kewpie and I quit at four and there was still a crowd. My arms and hands ached from whaling away at the box and my head ached worse from hearing Kewpie sing and play consistently out of tune. He had damned little more idea of pitch than an alley tom-cat. And Rucci had kept on bringing gals over and introducing me but hadn't brought any of the Wendel crowd.

He'd tried to please; I'll give him that. He kept sending out to the bar for drinks for Kewpie and me until I told him plenty. I hadn't lied; one hell of a lot of the customers had done the same and we didn't want to take a shingle from the roof and tell them no. Kewpie and I cut thirty-one dollars and sixty cents, which wasn't bad for a week night, and he said: "You see, Shean! I told you this was a good spot and it is. Kewpie knows, by God! We'll do better over the week-end always, and when we get a live one in we'll really go to town. Wait until Monday night."

"Why wait until Monday?" I asked.

He grinned and said: "It ain't any different than any [' other sporting town, Shean. A bunch of the gals lay off on Monday, because it's a slack night for them, and they give the spot a play. A lot of them will hustle a John who's good for dough and bring him along. And any dumb prostitute will spend as much as a dozen business men herself. You know that."

I said I had that recollection, even though I'd been out of the business for a little while. We ate, then drove back to If the hotel, and Kewpie walked on to the rooming house he was honoring, after telling me he'd drop up and see me around noon the next day.

I parked the car and went up to the room and didn't find Lester. He'd left the club around two and he'd told me he was going to take the big bum home, then go to bed. He'd had about five more drinks than he could really hold and I'd told him it was a good idea. Just about the time I'd decided to call the desk and find out if the big gal was registered in the hotel, he came in.

He'd been pretty well plastered when he left the club and now he really had a load. I looked at him and said:

"Well, well! And you the boy that doesn't believe in drinking. Maybe it was something you ate."

He didn't answer me. He just waved his hands in front of his face and stumbled for the bathroom. I followed him in and kept him from taking a header while he heaved, then said: "This ought to be a lesson, kid. You're just one of the kind that can't take it. This ought to show you."

He said, in an all-gone voice: "I couldn't help it, Shean. She kept saying 'Let's have another one, honey' and what could I say? I couldn't very well tell her I didn't believe in drinking."

"Why not?" He managed to straighten up a little. "It wouldn't have been polite."

I'd been trying to keep from laughing, but this was too much. I asked: "Did you slap her face, or were you too drunk?"

He looked puzzled and asked what that meant. I said: "Hell! Usually when I'm trying to make a gal and get her too drunk she passes out on me. If she don't get that drunk, she's still sober enough to slap my face. Did you give in?"

He said: "My God, Shean! I'm sick! Don't rib me now. I can't stand it!"

I said: "That's just *your* notion," and proved him wrong during the time it took him to get to bed. This was about an hour. He'd get a shoe off and then have to make another run. He undressed in sections, as it were. I felt sorry for him, but I laid the lash on his back just the same.

He'd bawled me out for hangovers too many times. Though, of course, always in a polite way.

CHAPTER SEVEN

Kirby called me at ten the next morning. I answered the phone and he said: "This is John Kirby. How about coming down for a little while?"

I said I could, as soon as I was dressed. He said that was fine and hung up, and Lester rolled over in bed and groaned:

"Who was that?"

I said: "The Chief, is all. Your Mrs. Heber has gone down and lodged a complaint against you."

He came wide awake. He sat up in bed and said:

"WHAT!"

"Sure! You might have known. You can't get tough with a woman in this town and get away with it."

"But Shean! I didn't do anything."

"How in hell do you know you didn't? You were so stiff when you got home I could have propped you up against the wall. That happens lots of times, Lester. A man will do things and not remember them."

I kept this up while I got dressed and I just about had him believing me by the time I'd finished. He was almost crying by then, and he said, just when I went out:

"Shean, I didn't do anything. Honest, I didn't."

I said: "That's the beef, you clown," and slammed the door. It was a shame to ride him but too good a chance to miss.

Kirby wasn't alone when I got to the station. He had a lantern-jawed, gabled-shouldered man with him whom lie introduced as Len MacIntosh. He added: "Len's with the Sheriff, Connell. We work together pretty well."

I said I was glad to meet Mr. MacIntosh, even though I didn't know whether I meant it or not, and took a seat across the desk from the two of them. Kirby tossed a telegram across to me and said:

"From New York. They get action back there, those boys do. Twenty-four hours for this is all."

The wire read FRANCINE DEBREAUX ARRIVED JULY THIRTY-TWO STOP TWICE MARRIED STOP WORKED FOR G L STODDARD STOP DISMISSED FOR THEFT STOP WORKED FOR GEORGE ARM-BRUSTER STOP ARRESTED FOR THEFT STOP TWO YEAR

TERM IN BEDFORD STOP SERVED FIFTEEN MONTHS STOP NO
FURTHER RECORD STOP REFERENCES GIVEN US FALSE STOP

It was signed by somebody in the Identification Bureau. I said:
"That's nice work, Chief. It's a wonder she wasn't deported."

"They don't deport them that easily," he said. "Chances are,
nobody thought it was worth the bother. D'ya notice that bit about
references?"

I said: "That would be a cinch for her. She probably made
some connection while she was in the gow. Forged references
would be a cinch and the average person doesn't bother to check
them."

Kirby picked up the phone and called a number. He asked to
speak to Mrs. Ruth Wendel, got her after a wait, and asked: "Mrs.
Wendel. Did you bother to check your maid's references before you
hired her a year ago? I have a reason for asking."

There was another wait, then I could hear tinny sounds
coming from the phone. Kirby said: "Thank you!" hung up the
receiver and told me:

"She says she didn't bother. That the girl seemed careful and
competent and she just didn't bother."

I said: "Okey, then you've got it. She had fake references. But
now you got it what does it mean?"

He said slowly: "It means this. This French maid was a crook.
Or at least she'd been one. Maybe some person she'd crossed back
in New York followed her out here and knifed her. Maybe she'd had
an affair with the knife man back there and the guy followed her.
It's something to go on."

"I can't see it," I argued. "I don't blame you for passing the
buck back to New York but I can't see it. It's a local mess, I think."

"We've checked that woman for the time she's been here and
she wasn't out with a soul. That's out. She made no contacts that
could lead to murder. Isn't that right, Len?"

Len MacIntosh said that was right; that his office had assisted
in the check and the Debreaux woman had met no one and had
gone out with no one. He reached in his pocket for cigarettes,
passed the package to me and said:

"Have one?"

I looked and saw they were Turkish, the kind the young gals
smoke when they want to be devilish. I said no, that I always
smoked my own kind, and the long lean hungry-looking bird said:
"I can't sand those. I have to have them mild like these. Never
smoke any other kind."

This, with him looking like the breath of the old West, mind you.

Kirby said thoughtfully: "I wanted to tell you this, Connell, because I think Wendel is mixed up with this murder someway. I know you're in the clear, of course. But I don't know anything about him."

I said: "My good God! The poor devil's nuts about his wife. That's all that's the matter with him. He couldn't have murdered this girl; he was at the same party I was, at the time it happened. You can check it."

"I have," Kirby admitted.

MacIntosh took a long drag at his cigarette and burst forth. "You've backed up my theory, Connell. You admit Wendel loves his wife. Now I say he had an affair with this maid and his wife found it out. That's why she's out here divorcing him. So he had this girl killed to keep her quiet; so his wife couldn't divorce him."

I laughed and said: "And I suppose the wife would keep the gal on her payroll, knowing her old man was having an affair with her? That won't hold up. She'd fire her the second she knew it."

"Maybe she wanted the girl as a witness and kept her along on that account. That holds water, doesn't it?"

"Now look and remember," I said. "You saw that girl. She wasn't pretty. Mrs. Wendell is. I know that a guy will go for a homely girl lots of times, but not this time. Not this guy. This Wendel was no party hound and never was. He ain't the type to chase women."

Kirby asked: "How d'ya know that?"

"Joey Free told me. He went to school with Wendel. They're pals. He told me Wendel was safe and sane at all times."

Kirby said: "Hell! He's human, ain't he. He's safe and sane like Fourth of July celebrations are. I notice people still get hurt at them. You can't change human nature."

I said: "That's my argument. A play like that wouldn't be in Wendel's nature. He's a dope."

We argued about it some more and Kirby asked if I'd seen Mrs. Wendel. I said I hadn't; that I'd made no attempt at seeing her. That I could take a gentle hint without having both shins kicked black and blue. He grinned over at MacIntosh and said: "I told you he was half smart."

MacIntosh said: "Or maybe just canny," and on that note I left.

Breakfast was to be a three-way affair; Lester, Kewpie, and I, so I stopped in the same Rustic Bar for a drink on the way back to the hotel. I had plenty of time and I'd had enough to drink the night before to need one. I got inside and to the bar and told the smug-looking bird behind it what I wanted and happened to look out on the street. There was a Cadillac coupe going by and I could have sworn I saw Joey Free back of the wheel. I didn't think anything about it at the time, feeling sure that Joey was in the City then, but when I got back to the hotel and Lester said: "Miss Gahagen called and wants you to call her," I thought maybe something had come up at that end and that Joey had driven up to tell me about it personally.

I got Long Distance, and finally the Gahagan and said:

"This is me. What's the matter?"

She said: "You told me to call you if anything came up. That's what I did."

I could hear her giggle over the phone. "Oh nothing much. Do you remember giving me a check for a hundred dollars to put in your personal account?"

"Sure. Joey Free's."

"Well, it bounced. No funds."

"You're nuts, Red. He's good."

"You're nuts if you think I'm nuts," she said. "He may good but his checks bounced just the same. D'ya want protest it?"

"Hell, no. He's good, I tell you. There's some mistake."

"Well, that's the reason I called you. How long you going to stay there?"

"I've got a job, Red. Maybe forever."

She laughed and said: "A break for me! You can't stay longer than six weeks on that expense account. You've been up there two days; that leaves you forty more."

I didn't get it and said so. She said: "It's simple. That woman will get her divorce after she's there six weeks. Forty-two days. I take it that's what Wendel doesn't want. He's lot going to pay you after she gets it, is he?"

I said: "This is costing me money," and hung up. And then called back. I got her in five minutes and said:

"Listen, Red! Call up Joey's apartment and find out if he's there. I mean in town. Get it? Then write me a letter about it and send it air mail. I'll get it in the morning."

She said she understood.

I told Lester about thinking I'd seen Joey driving by. He put on his thoughtful look and said: "That seems hardly logical, Shean. I mean, after all, with the police chasing him out and all. He'd hardly turn around and come back, would he?"

I said I'd thought of that myself. The telephone rang then and I picked it up, thinking it would be Kewpie calling from the lobby. A very soft, sweet, and feminine voice said:

"Is it you, honey?"

I told her that I wasn't sure but that it might just possibly be, and the voice froze up and snapped: "I would like to speak to Mr. Lester Hoyt."

I said to Lester: "It's your honey."

He talked and I gathered she was trying to rope him into a car ride, far into the romantic mountains. Where the old hills could look down on young love and so on. I kept snickering and he kept getting redder and redder in the face and his stalling kept getting weaker. Finally I said:

"Tell the old itch-bay you'll go. What the hell! You only live once and she hasn't got so many more years." He told her he'd meet her in the lobby in twenty minutes, then told me: "You shouldn't say things like that about her, Shean! She's really very nice."

"Sure. I bet she has you carrying matches pretty soon."

"She's lonesome. She knows very few people here."

"Okey, kid! She's the motherly type, I guess. She's old enough to be yours."

He left the room on that one and I decided I'd have a talk with the old gal if I ever got her by herself. After all, I felt responsible for Lester though I couldn't see much harm in his running around with her as long as he didn't marry her.

That would be *too* tough for him. Number four on her list at *his* age. I believe in anybody getting experience... but not in too big doses.

CHAPTER EIGHT

Kewpie and I had breakfast and stalled around until time to go to work. Most of the time I talked with Kewpie about getting that soggy sax tone of his up half a notch and he didn't like it much. Probably no more than I liked the soggy tone he had. We went out to the place about seven and Gino Rucci met us, beaming all over, and said to me: "I would like to speak to you."

We went off to the side and he nodded at Kewpie and said: "Do you suppose you can find another man in his place? The people, they like you; they do not like him."

It didn't make any difference to me, but Kewpie had tried to give me a break and I appreciated it. I said: "That's out. I work with Kewpie or I don't work. And I don't give a damn whether I work or not."

He started waving his hands and saying it was all a mistake. I calmed down and so did he. Finally he said:

"You like the girls I introduce you to last night? Nice girls, are they."

I spit it out at him. "I'd like to meet the one you didn't introduce. The one in that party you were sitting with last night."

"That is the Mrs. Wendel. She's ah ... she's..."

He tried to think of a word and I watched his eyes. Usually they were soft and brown and good-natured, but now they looked as though a shade had been pulled over them. Glazed. I said: "Oh, no difference. She was pretty, though."

He beamed again. "Very pretty. Very good customer. She comes out with Crandall. Mister Crandall is a lawyer; a very good one."

I said was that right and went back to Kewpie. There was nobody in back, so we went out to the bar in front and I said to him: "What kind of a guy is this Rucci? He seems like a good Joe."

"He's a smart egg, Shean! He's made money when there's been others starved. He'll shoot all angles."

"Hustler, hunh?"

Kewpie laughed. "You should ask. That soft soap of his don't fool anybody. He owns a good half of the town. No, not that much dough, but he's well fixed and then some. Part of two banks. This place. A cut in two of the gambling places down town. He's got a piece of the Rustic, that bar where I first met you. He's got a dude ranch out in the country and a couple of mines. Rucci is no slouch."

I said it would seem not. I said: "He seems friendly with Crandall."

"Crandall's his lawyer, same as he's the lawyer for most of the money men in town. Crandall's good I guess; I don't know him."

I said: "Lawyers are good people to stay away from. Let's get to work."

Crandall and Mrs. Wendel, the two guards and the two the-less-said-the-betters came in about ten and Rucci led them to a booth almost facing the piano. We had a nice crowd and I was working hard but I still could notice Rucci talking and waving his hands and nodding toward me. Finally Crandall and Mrs. Wendel danced and Rucci came over to the piano. He flagged them down when they pranced by and said: "Mr. Crandall! Mrs. Wendel! I want you to meet Shean Connell."

I nodded, and kept on playing. Crandall said: "Come on over to the booth and have a drink with us when you get a chance."

I said thank you... and took them up on it half an hour later.

Crandall was nice... too nice. Mrs. Wendel acted as though I wasn't on earth, beyond saying: "Hello!" when I first went over. It wasn't that she high-hatted me; she just ignored me. I was as the dirt under her feet, if actions meant a thing. The two guards were very guarded, saying not a hell of a lot more than she did. The two chippies were swarming over me like bees... and I'd just as soon have had the bees.

I left for the next set of tunes and Rucci came over and shrugged and said: "She is like that, that lady. Very dignified. Very high class. She is rich; she has the guards with her at all times in case of trouble."

"What kind of trouble?"

He shrugged again. "Hold-ups, kidnapping, anything may happen to the very rich."

That was the size of it. The Wendel party left about two, the same as the night before. We quit about four and I went home to find Lester in bed and asleep. Which was rather a surprise; I'd thought his big mama was going to do better than that on her second time out with him.

The three of us, Kewpie, Lester, and I, were eating breakfast the next morning when I looked over at another table and saw Bill Maxwell and Charley Howard. I said to Lester: "Well, good Lord!

Two pals. Excuse me."

Lester said: "Sure. I've got a date this afternoon, Shean, so don't plan on me going with you anyplace."

I looked at Kewpie and winked and Kewpie looked puzzled. I said: "Those two guys I've known for ten years. They're card dealers. I used to know them when I worked in Eureka. They had a pan game there."

"Pan game?" Lester asked.

"Panguingi. It's like rummy, only more so. Like a cross between rummy and coon-can. It's insanity and slow death. You can't quit playing it once you start and the house gets all the money because they're cutting the game so hard."

Lester lied and said: "I see!" and Kewpie laughed and said: "I've played it. I never had a dime all the time I did."

I went over and said hello to Bill and Charley and they said they were working at the Bank Club, Bill at the Faro bank and Charley back of the crap layout. Lester and Kewpie came over, Lester to tell me he was going back to the hotel and his date, and Kewpie to say he had to see a man about a dog. I waited until Bill and Charley got through eating, then said: "Come out and see me at the Three C Club. I'm working out there."

They said they would and we walked down the street together. We got almost level with the first National Bank, and I saw Ruth Wendel and the same two guards come out and start toward us. I said:

"Hello!" to the three of them, smiling, and the two guards grunted and stepped in close to her. She looked right through me and kept walking. Bill and Charley and I stared after them, and Charley laughed and said:

"Madge is getting high-hat as hell. She never even spoke to me. I don't blame her for passing you up, Connell, but I used to know her old man."

"What d'ya mean, her old man?"

"Her old man. She's Madge Giovanatti. She used to be with Harry Kieth, when he ran that joint on Post Street. That would be five, no six years ago. I guess maybe she's forgotten me."

Bill Maxwell said: "I couldn't blame her for that."

I said: "You're screwy, Charley. That's Mrs. Ruth Wendel from New York City. I met her last night. She's got dough in lots. Here for a divorce."

Charley grinned and said: "Maybe that's why she didn't speak to me. I don't know any New York society women, but this one looks like Madge Giovanatti, I swear."

"She didn't speak to me, either, and I just met her last night. She acted as though she didn't think much of me then."

Bill said again: "And I couldn't blame her for that." They dropped me at the hotel and I told them I'd look in on their games, later on. I went inside, found I'd had no calls and read the city papers through. Then I went down to the Bank Club.

I'd dropped sixty dollars on Bill's faro bank, and spent four hours doing it, when I felt a tap on my shoulder. I wasn't feeling good about losing the dough, and I swung around and said: "What's the matter?"

It was Kirby, and he didn't look as pleasant as he usually did. He said: "I want to talk to you, Connell. Cash in."

"Suppose I go down to the station after a while? I want to get well. I'm in the game now and it can't go on like this forever."

Kirby grinned, but not with any humor in the grin, and said: "Hell, I'm doing you a favor. You'll get sicker. You can't beat the bank unless you're right. Come on now."

I said to Bill Maxwell: "The law's got me, Bill. I'll be back after my sixty pretty soon."

"I'll save it for you," he said, and I followed Kirby out to the street and to his car. I was a bit hot under the collar ... I'd a hunch that I was going to start calling the turn about that time. I said:

"Couldn't this wait, Chief? I hate like hell to have to quit right now. On top of that, I don't like to have a cop take me out of a place, now or any other time."

"It can't wait," he said.

He drove down to the station and neither of us said a word until we were inside. Len McIntosh was in the Chief's office, waiting for us, and he drawled out: "Hello, Connell!" I said hello and took my usual seat. Kirby took his and started out with: "I tried to give you a break, Connell, and one for myself along with you. You don't want to play it that way, hunh?"

"What d'ya mean?"

"I gave you the dope once. I figured you'd play smart, stick here a while and make yourself a fee out of this Wendel. Instead, you bull ahead and put yourself in bad. And me on the pan. I won't go for that."

This had me down and I asked him what he meant. He said impatiently: "You know damned well what I mean. You try and bust into that woman on the street and she makes a complaint about it. I understand you wangled an introduction to her last night and I can't stop that. But this street business! Insisting on talking to her when she doesn't want to talk to you! That I can and will stop."

I said: "Now, wait a minute!" and told him just exactly what had happened. That I'd said hello and that was all. That I'd been with two friends, who'd tell him the same if he'd ask them. I said: "It's like this. I'm here and minding my business. It's your town and I know it. But I'm damned if I'm going to get railroaded out of it over a thing like this. There's something screwy about this."

Len MacIntosh said: "Sure there's something screwy about this. There's a murder and murder's screwy to say the least. This time and every time."

Kirby said: "Crandall called me and said you'd annoyed Mrs. Wendell on the street. If you keep on with this, Connell, hell have you bound over under a peace bond and it will be a heavy one. That's what he said, if it means anything. He can do it."

I said: "He told you what to do and you're doing it. I catch."

He got a dull red, and said stubbornly: "I told you how I stand heife. You know the set-up. Why make it tough for me?"

I said: "Am I supposed to be arrested?"

"No."

"Then I'm leaving. You know where you can find me."

"It won't be at the Three C Club," MacIntosh said, grinning.

"Why not?"

"Crandall said not, over the phone. I guess he doesn't want to leave you any reason for sticking around town."

I said to both of them: "Either of you tell Crandall why I'm in town?"

MacIntosh shook his head and Kirby said: "I never told a soul. Not even my old lady. I keep the office and gossip apart, if you know what I mean."

"I told nobody, either," MacIntosh said. "But Crandall knows I'm a cop that's trying to talk to Mrs. Wendel. Isn't that it?"

Kirby said slowly: "He didn't say that. But I wouldn't bet he didn't know. He gets around; he hears things. I've heard the same thing, for that matter. That you're a shamus, that is. I didn't hear what you were here for."

"Who told you?"

He thought a moment, said: "As I remember, the bar man in the Rustic Grill. He said something about you not taking a drink with me, that day I met you there. It was some ribbing remark about a private cop being too good to drink with the city force. I didn't pay any attention; I didn't know it was supposed to be a secret."

I said: "At that time I didn't either. It's no secret now, I can see that."

I left there, boiling. Kirby wasn't the type to shoot his mouth off about anybody else's business and I didn't think MacIntosh was, either. Kewpie didn't know a thing and so I couldn't blame it on him.

That left Lester. And the kid might well have made some remark to that big blonde mama of his and spilled the beans. I started back to the hotel to wait for him... and I spent the time it took me to get there thinking about the things I was going to say to him.

CHAPTER NINE

Just before I got to the hotel I had to pass a newsstand, and I stopped there to get something to read while waiting for Lester. The magazines were spread out by the stand on a sort of platform for display and there was a brick wall back of the platform. Just the space between two stores. I got what I wanted and started to turn back to the stand to pay and something flicked the top of my ear as I did. And right then a brick in front of me spattered red dust.

I heard the gun then but until I'd put my hand up to my ear and brought it down and looked at the blood on it I didn't realize what the sound had been. It hadn't been loud; about like the noise a heavy whip makes when cracked.

It didn't occur to me the slug had been aimed my way. Not in that second. But another brick, just at the side of the one already hit, chipped with another bullet and I got smart to what was going on.

I heard the sound again as I turned and ran. I ducked into the corner store... the door wasn't more than ten feet away... and stopped inside the shadow and looked across the street.

There was a rooming house there, set above the one story store buildings. Half the windows were open and there wasn't a way in the world of telling from which one the shot had been fired. I walked through the place, holding my hand up to my ear and stopping most of the blood, went out the side door and into the first drug store I ran into. I told the druggist: "I've hurt my ear. Can you put a plaster on it?"

I took my hand away, letting blood pour all over the shoulder of my coat, and he said: "You ought to go to a doctor, man!"

"Patch it up so I can."

He led me into the back room and swabbed the ear with some antiseptic that burned like so much fire, then asked:

"How did you do it?"

"I didn't," I said.

"What happened, mister?"

I said: "As near as I can figure, some kid accidentally fired a twenty-two and I got in the way of it."

He shook his head. "These damn kids. Their folks hadn't

ought to allow them to have guns. Guns are bad medicine for kids to have."

I said that was right and thought he shouldn't single out kids on the gun-owning business. I didn't think any kid had owned the gun that had dusted the bricks in front of me.

He patched up the ear with tape and said: "It isn't as bad as I thought, mister. There's about half an inch of the top gone but it's taken off clean. I'd go to a doctor, though, just to be sure. I can patch you up in an emergency like this, but I'm no M. D."

I thanked him and paid him and went in the side door of the hotel. And for the first time noticed I still had the magazine I'd picked out and hadn't paid for. I'm willing to bet that newsstand man figured I'd put on an act for his benefit but the Lord knows I hadn't ... it had been entirely for my own.

Lester got back to the room about half an hour after I did. He came in, looking guilty, and I said: "Well, did you give in yet? Are you hers and hers alone?"

He said: "No!" looked at me and the tape on my head, and said:: "What's happened?"

"A guy shot me is all."

"What for?"

"I'm trying to figure it out. I don't know any reason anybody should try to do me in."

He was jumping up and down and making motions with his arms. He dashed over to the phone, started to pick it up, and I took it away from him and said: "What are you going to do?"

"Call the police, of course."

"I've talked to Kirby already."

"Is he after the man that shot you?" I said: "Listen, Lester! Use your head! I don't know the man who shot me and I've no way of finding out who he is. At least, not right this minute. What chance has Kirby got? Why bother *him* about it?"

"What did you talk to him about?"

"He wants me to get out of town. At least he more than hinted that's what he wanted. It seems I've lost my job and that I'm not wanted here any more."

"Why did you lose your job?"

"Mr. Crandall doesn't like me. That's the only thing I can think."

He sat down on the edge of the bed and watched me take another drink. It was the third I'd had since being in the room and I'd lost part of my peeve. He said, seriously:

"Did you ever think, Shean, getting that job the way you did was sort of funny? You know, just walking into it like that."

I had and it had been bothering me, puzzling me. But I said: "That's nothing. The guy was stuck for a piano player and had to have one. That often happens."

"That's a better job than most of them around here, isn't it?"

"Sure. There's no money in that business any more."

"Then why wouldn't some other piano player have heard about it and quit his job and taken that one? Why wouldn't he?"

I didn't know and said so. Lester said: "I don't know but I don't like Kewpie. I think maybe there's something wrong with him."

"Sure there is. He's too fat."

"I don't mean that way."

"Use your head," I said. "Kewpie ran into me at the Rustic Bar, not even knowing I was in town. He'd heard this job was open out there and thought I was still in the music business. So he told me about it. How can you make anything out of that? And why would he? Why would anybody want me to take a piano job out there? How would anybody know I wanted to meet Mrs. Wendel and think that was a good way to do it? Tell me that."

"Suppose he knew you were in town and just pretended to run into you? What about that?"

"How would he know? Don't be silly, Lester."

Lester said darkly: "There's something funny about this matter," and I said: "You're damned right there is, now that you bring it up. I'll tell you. You cracked to this blonde bitch about who I was and what I was here for and she's passed it on. Now don't tell me you didn't; I know you did."

He opened his eyes wide, taking off his glasses and goggling at me like an owl. "But, Shean, I did no such thing. I told her I was a college man, just up here for atmosphere. That I was writing a thesis on the divorce problem."

"You let it slip, kid. You must have. How could it have gotten out if you hadn't?"

"I didn't. I know I-didn't."

"What about night before last when you got so lousy drunk? You could have told her anything and not have known what you were saying."

He hung his head and said that he'd been drunk but that he didn't think he'd said anything about it. I said: "It's a cinch. And she's passed it on to Crandall or Mrs. Wendel or to somebody that's passed it to them."

He said, surprisingly: "Didn't I tell you? She knows Crandall and Mrs. Wendel. She was here two weeks before Mrs. Wendel and she met her the first day Mrs. Wendel got here. Crandall's her lawyer, too."

"Well, there you are."

He almost cried and I read him a blistering lecture about going out with big blonde women and getting drunk and making a fool of himself. This was funny, coming from me. I'd made a fool of myself over big blondes and little blondes as well as every other different kind of gal all my life. I had no reason to talk but he was in no position to point that out. Or in no mood. Finally I laid off the flaying and he quit saying he was sorry about everything, including living, and I took another drink and things got back to normal.

Then he handed me a letter and said: "This was downstairs. The clerk said it just came in."

The letter was from the Gahagan, back in the office. The first of it was a report on some routine work I'd done about checking on a bird that started bad store accounts and skipped out of town. I hadn't done much good on the thing, but had found that he'd come from Portland, Oregon, and tipped the police there to watch for him. They'd caught him, which meant we'd get a fee from the department store and no argument with it. Good news.

And then she went on with some not so good. Joey Free's check had bounced and she was going to try it again in a few days. She'd called Joey's apartment and he hadn't been there. Wendel had answered the phone and told her Joey had gone to Los Angeles for three or four days and that he was holding the fort. Naturally, she hadn't said a word to Wendel about Joey's check coming back on us. She said Free had called Wendel that same morning, from Los Angeles, and had said he'd be back in three or four days, and that Wendel had said he'd stick close to Free's apartment, in case I wanted to get in touch with him about anything. I winked at Lester, got Long Distance, and said:

"I'd like to speak to Mr. Todhunter Wendel, at Mr. Joey Free's apartment in San Francisco. Rush this through sister, and I'll send you a box of candy; I'm on an expense account."

She said: "I like flowers better; I'm on a diet. D'ya know the number of Mr. Free's apartment?"

I said I didn't. She said: "I'll look it up, Mr. Connell. Anything for you... and the flowers."

Lester muttered, sotto voce: "I'll bet she's blonde," and I said: "Forget it, kid! I'm a little upset right now. I don't like to get shot at."

"Shean, that's something. You said you thought it was a .22. Would anybody trying to kill a man use a gun that small?"

"It was a .22 rifle, kid. At a distance like that, a good shot can damned near drive tacks with one. They don't make much noise and with this new high-speed stuff they burn in them now, they'd kill a man as quick as a cannon. That is, if they hit him in the head. Both slugs were at head level."

"I thought gangsters used revolvers mostly."

This was funny and struck me that way. "It doesn't make any difference what's used to kill a man if it does the business, does it? He's just as dead."

Lester agreed this was reasonable. I said: "D'ya think this big amp-tray of yours could find out what the Wendel woman is getting a divorce for? Why her husband can't see her? How's that for an angle?"

Lester said doubtfully: "Well, I guess I could ask her. I could ask her to find out, that is."

"Let it go," I said, as fast as I could.

The phone rang and the Long Distance girl said: "I like almost any kind of flowers, Mr. Connell. Here's your party," and then after the usual amount of clicking back and forth, Wendel said: "Hello! Hello!"

I said: "This is Connell. In Reno."

"Oh yes, Connell."

"Where's Joey Free?"

"In Los Angeles. He called me from there last night and this morning. I'll ask for his address there when he calls again."

"Never mind. Who's your lawyer here?"

"I haven't one."

"Wire whoever you've got in New York, then, and have them get somebody here to represent you. Anybody but Crandall, tell them. That's customary. And do it in a hurry and let me know. Is that clear?"

"Of course. I'll do it at once. How are you coming along? Have you talked with her?"

"Yeah, but I haven't found anything out yet. This is tough; it takes time."

I could hear him groan and then he said: "You haven't much time, Connell. She's been there over two weeks already."

"I've got four more. What d'ya know about your wife's maid?"

"Why, nothing at all. Ruth seemed to think she was very

satisfactory. Wasn't that terrible?"

"Didn't anybody ask you and Joey questions about her?"

"A few. I couldn't see any connection between the maid and myself and said so, naturally."

I said: "Okey! Get that dope and shoot it to me in a hurry. All right?"

He said all right and I hung up. The minute I did Lester said: "What did you mean, let it go? Why shouldn't I ask Hazel to see Mrs. Wendel?"

"I'm afraid you'd botch it up."

"I'm smart enough not to do that," he said proudly.

I said I wasn't so sure, and then: "D'ya suppose she's got a friend that would like to party? The four of us, I mean."

"I don't know."

I dug out an envelope I'd happened to have in my pocket when I was working at the Club, and said: "Let that go, too. The only thing is, ask her if she'd like to go out tonight."

He said: "I've got a date already."

I said: "You would. You're that sheik type," and got busy on the phone.

I had four numbers and began to believe I was going to draw a blank. The first two girls I called were busy that night. But the third said she'd just love to go out and so on and I said I'd call for her at eight. I'd taken the numbers more from habit than anything else and couldn't remember just which one of the many Rucci had introduced me to she was, but I figured I'd know her when I met her. I got the house doctor up and had a bit neater job done on my sore ear, and he was just leaving when Kewpie came in.

Kewpie looked glum and said: "We lost out some way at the Club. Rucci told me had made other arrangements. I meauwed about us getting no notice and he said that was just too bad and for me to take it up with the union. Hell, I didn't put in my card when I came. I've been here three months and nobody's asked me for one."

I said: "No need of us going out then," and shook my head at Lester, meaning for him to say nothing.

He got the idea, for once, and didn't. Kewpie looked thoughtfully after the doctor, then at my taped ear, and said:

"Didn't hit you bad, eh?"

"What d'ya mean?"

"So you won't talk. I heard about it and wondered if you were going to crack, is all. I heard that somebody got shot at on the street.

"Where'd you hear it?"

I was worried by then. I thought maybe it was common gossip. He made it all right when he said: "I know the news dealer where it happened. He'd seen you and me together and told me about it. He said you'd been gone five minutes before he figured what had happened and that you owed him two bits for the Cosmopolitan you'd taken with you."

"Did you pay it?"

"*I* should pay your bills."

I told him what had happened, blaming it on some kid playing around not knowing what he was doing, and Kewpie said: "Sure, that's your story. I won't crack, Shean, but I saw those two bricks. Some bastard was aiming for your head and you can't tell me different."

"Maybe so, Kewpie. I don't know why." He said earnestly: "Now look, Shean! You and I have worked together a couple of times. I've known you quite a while. If I can help, I'll do it and you know it." I said: "I catch!"

Lester had been listening to this. He poured out two drinks, one for me and one for Kewpie, and said: "Here you are," beaming at both of us.

It was right about that time that he decided Kewpie was a good guy; I could have told him that and did, all the time. You learn about people when you work with them.

CHAPTER TEN

My girl turned out to be a Spanish-looking brunette. Very snaky and very pretty. But she talked as though her mouth were full of mush, which spoiled the effect, and I wished to God I'd tried the fourth number on the list before I'd tried hers. Mrs. Hazel George-Wolff-Heber was about as I had her picked. Just a big good-natured wench that couldn't keep her hands off any man, regardless of size, age, or color. She kept telling Lester that she adored men who wore glasses, because they looked so distinguished. She told me she adored music and musicians. She made pig eyes at the good-looking cab driver who drove us out to the Three C Club and she did everything but climb over the bar after the bar man who served us the first drink when we got there.

Just a good kid... but a bit worn. I couldn't tell whether the gargling effect my tart put on or Hazel's giggles were the worse; both got on my nerves before we'd got once around the track.

We moved in the back room and took a look at the man that followed me on the job, and Hazel leaned over and patted me on the cheek and said: "He doesn't play half as well as you do, honey. Tee-hee-hee!"

Lester said the same, very loyally. My bitch, who gargled, yessed on it. For that matter, I didn't think he did myself, so we were all even. Then Rucci came over to the booth, smiling and shaking his head, and said:

"Why, Connell! I was told you were leaving. I hired this other man in your place, as I told Kewpie."

"Who told you?" I asked.

He made a pretense of trying to remember and finally said he *didn't* remember; that he'd been around all that day and had met so many people. He'd hired the new man to be sure he'd have music and so on. He was very nice... too nice... and brought a round of drinks before he hurried away.

The phone booths were by the hall leading to the men's room and as soon as he dashed into one I made the sneak. He hadn't the door quite closed when I went by and I could hear him say to somebody: "I tell you he's here now. Right now. In a party. There's the Heber, that kid,..."

I couldn't stand there and listen so I went on. I went back to the booth and by and by the two girls went to powder their noses. I said to Lester:

"You wanted to be a cop, didn't you?"

He said: "Sure!" and took off his glasses and started to polish them. I said: "You'd better leave them on, kid, and get the hell out of here with these two women, or you're going to find out that a cop leads a hard life."

He brightened and said: "Is it trouble, Shean? Is it trouble?"

"With a capital *T*, I think. I'm on a spot."

He said firmly: "We'll send the girls home and I'll stay with you, of course. You should know that."

I said: "I know it. I told you because I knew I couldn't get rid of you just telling you to go and giving you no reason. At least you know what to expect."

"What will happen?"

I said: "Dope! Here it comes now."

Three men were heading for the booth, coming across the dance floor and walking as though they were more used to sawdust under their feet. All three looked like saloon bouncers. That type. The one in the lead was a big burly red-faced bird that would have weighed at least two-fifty stripped to the buff. We had two ashtrays, heavy glass affairs, on the table and I palmed the one nearest me and stood up and got clear of the booth. The big guy said:

"You're Connell!" out of the side of his mouth and he didn't make it any question.

I said: "Sure!" and hit him in the face with the tray.

That worked just fine and dandy. He went back and down, skidding across the floor and upsetting the one right back of him. The one left side-stepped them and came toward me fast, swinging something in his hand, and I got a couple of feet farther away from the booth so that I'd have room to work in. He cut at me with what he held and I saw it was a sap, even as he swung it. I got in closer than he thought I could in the time I had and I hit him just a little lower than the belly and as hard as I could land. *That* worked, also. He doubled up, dropping the sap, and I brought my knee up in his face. He went down and out.

And then I turned and saw something funny. Lester, without his glasses, can't see five feet from his face. And then he was crying and that didn't help his sight a bit. He'd managed to get clear of the booth and grapple with the second man, and grapple is just the word I mean. He had both arms around him and it looked as though he was trying to climb up him like a kid climbs a tree.

I'd dropped my tray when I'd hit the first one. I circled Lester and his partner, waited until I got a clear shot at the partner's jaw, and smacked.

He just shook his head and I wondered if I'd lost my punch. I circled around the two of them again, waiting for another chance, and then I heard a scream, right in my ear, and the Heber woman brought down a hefty handbag across the guy's head.

It hurt Lester more than it did the guy because he shook Lester off with a sort of wiggle. But it bothered him enough to make him stand still and I got him by the wrist and then turned and threw him over my shoulder. It wasn't hard. I yanked and stooped at the same time and he went over in the old flying mare. He landed in a heap and I got there and kicked him in the face before he could scramble up.

The first guy was out cold, with blood streaming from his face. The ashtray, with all my weight behind it, had caught him across the bridge of the nose. He was a mess.

The second was rolling around on the floor and holding his arms wrapped around the lower part of himself.

The third didn't look well either. He was lying flat on his back by the piano and the piano player was staring down at him as though he didn't believe what he was looking at.

I went back to the booth and said to the two women and Lester: "Let's get out of here! Quick! Or we'll be mobbed."

The Heber woman was crying out: "He was killing Lester! He was killing Lester!"

My Spanish-looking gal said: "My God, man! Will this happen wherever we go?" and I almost liked her then. Lester was fumbling around with his glasses, too excited to put them on and blind as a bat without them. I put them on for him and we started for the door. Rucci got in the way, just as we got to the door between the back room and dance floor and the bar, and I straight-armed him out of the way. He went whirling back and we got in the bar proper.

The first thing I saw was Crandall, standing at the bar and gawking at us. I said to Lester: "There'll be a cab outside. Grab it quick!"

And then I want to Crandall. I said: "It didn't work, mister, but don't give up."

He grinned at me and said: "I won't."

I started to pass at him and somebody grabbed my arm when it went back. I could see I was outclassed, that I couldn't whip the entire bar bunch, so I said:

"I'll be seeing you."

He nodded, keeping his grin, and I dashed outside.

Lester and the women were just climbing in a cab. There was always one sticking around outside, waiting for a sucker. I climbed in after them and told the hacker: "Wheel her, boy! They don't like us here." He grinned and said: "Yus, Chief!" and I saw it was the same good-looking kid that had driven us out there.

So did Hazel Heber. She leaned forward and cooed: "My, did you wait for us?"

He said: "Hell, no!" That stopped her. We kept on taking in the spots until about twelve and by that time I thought Hazel was drunk enough to tell the truth, if she knew it. I was half tight. My Spanish effect was lit like a chandelier. Lester was cold sober and watching his Hazel with fear on his face. We were in a booth in the Palace Bar, and I leaned across to Hazel and said: "Lester tells me you know the Wendel woman." She giggled and said: "Li'l Hazel knows everybody. Knows 'em all, she does. Don't she?"

"Sure, Hazel, sure you do. What's she like?"

"She's swell kid. 'At's all Hazel knows; swell kids. You're swell kid; I'm swell kid." She screwed up her face and focused on my Spanish. "She ain't swell kid. She's bum."

Spanish said: "Why you big horse!" in an outraged voice and lifted her hand to cuff her. I caught her arm and said under my breath: "Easy, honey lamb! She's just stiff."

Spanish said, in the same tone, which was high and carrying: "So'm I drunk. So're you drunk. Everybody's drunk. But I'm no bum."

Hazel wagged a finger at her and insisted: "You are too a bum. I guess I know a bum when I see a bum."

I wanted to laugh but this was business and no place for pleasure. I hustled Spanish off what she was sitting on and out of the booth and started her back to the Ladies Room. I said: "Look, kitten, go back and wash your face with cold water. Run cold water on your wrists. If you don't you'll never last out the night and we're just starting to have fun." This has been a good argument for as long as I can remember. She fell for it. She looked up at me and said, in that gargling voice: "You come with me, Lover."

"I can't go in the Ladies Room."

She admitted this seemed sensible and weaved toward the back of the place. I sat down opposite Hazel and said:

"You were telling me about Mrs. Wendel."

She frowned and said: "She's better than me, hunh? Is zat it?"

I said: "Hazel, you're the sun and the moon and the stars for me. You know that. Don't be silly. I was just wondering why this Wendel woman was getting a divorce."

"Her old man was mean, that's why. Jus' like all the men he was. Mean. Mean, tha's what he was."

"What did he do: beat her up?"

"Sure! Alla time. She tol' me. He used to swear at her and call her dirty whore and things like 'at. No woman stand that. No *womanly* woman stand that."

I though possibly she was getting her case and Ruth Wendel's a bit mixed in her mind. I asked: "What grounds are *you* suing on?"

She said proudly: "I got reasons, too, I have. Cruel and inhuman treatment. D'ya know what 'at man did to me?"

I said I didn't.

"Used to read paper at breakfast. Make me get up for it then read paper. Talked about bills all time. Front of people he talked. No woman stand that. No *womanly* woman stand that. *Right?*"

I said: "Right. And the Wendel gal is suing because her papa beat her up and called her dirty names?"

"Sure. She tol' me."

She pounded on the table and called for another drink; she was drinking double-Scotch highballs, and Lester said in a worried voice: "Hazel, don't you think you've had enough for a while? Wouldn't it be better if you laid off?"

"Li'l Hazel *never* has enough. Not ever."

I said to Lester: "Well, every man has his cross to bear," and then my Spanish honey came staggering back and gasped: "Jesus, Honey, I'm sick," to me.

She sounded sick, but a hell of a lot soberer.

I said: "Let's get to hell out of here and let young love have a chance."

She gave me one of those kind of looks and said: "We can have a drink at my place. I want to lie down."

Lester made a frantic attempt at getting his blonde menace on his feet, so they could go with us, but it was hopeless. The big tramp sat solidly on what she had plenty of and wouldn't turn a wheel. The last I saw of them she was up-ping another Scotch and Lester was staring after me with a pained and worried expression.

My girl sobered up in the cab going home, enough to be more than a little sore when I wouldn't go in her apartment with her. I said: "Now look, hon! I've got a busy day tomorrow. I'll give you a ring during the afternoon."

She said: "Don't bother."

"Make it easy on yourself," I said, and turned and started down the hall, but she paddled after me and purred: "Don't you be mad at me, Sweet. You call me tomorrow afternoon."

"Sure, Pet."

"I'll wait by the phone for you to call."

I left, hoping she wouldn't go hungry sitting by the phone and waiting for me to call. She was pretty but I didn't like her voice. I don't expect 'em perfect, at my age, but I don't want them saying sweet nothings in my ear and sounding as though they had adenoids while they do it. It's not that I'm so fussy but you can hear a voice, even in the dark.

CHAPTER ELEVEN

Wendel had a long night letter waiting for me the next morning and I found out later he hadn't waited to wire New York but had called them on the phone. It said that his New York lawyers had advised him to consult Amos Mard, and that he was wiring Mard that I'd call to see him. That Mard and I should talk the situation over and decide what was best. And that I should keep in touch with him. I got on the phone, got Mard, and made an appointment for an hour from then, which barely left me time to dress and eat. Lester said, as I started out:

"I'd advise you to make sure Mard and Crandall aren't too friendly. They might work together on this."

I had a headache and a hangover and I snapped back: "You should tell me my business."

He grinned and said: "Okey, Shean," and I apologized for the temper and left.

Amos Mard was a young fellow, barely thirty. Or so I thought. We talked for a bit, with me being careful not to say anything that might carry to the enemy camp, until finally he said:

"You know, Mr. Connell, this is a bit unusual. Your coming to me like this. Frankly, there's something wrong with the case, though I don't know what it is. I sense that. If it wasn't that I have personal reasons, I'd turn it down."

"Does that mean you don't like Crandall?"

He shrugged and didn't answer but he'd said plenty. Unless Crandall threw things his way, Crandall would naturally be tough competition and a bad enemy for a young lawyer starting a practice. And Crandall didn't look to be the type to throw anything anybody's way unless there was more thrown back to him.

I said: "Okey, Mard, I guess I can let down my hair. Suppose we get down to cases. You'll be bucking Crandall and Gino Rucci and Christ knows who else. There's something screwy about the thing; there has been, right from the first."

"Why do you think Rucci is interested?"

"He's either a good enough friend of Crandall's to take up the hatchet for him, or he's getting a cut. I'd say the last; money's a better reason for him being in this than anything else. The case is built on money, as I see it."

"Why?"

He was doing the lawyer trick; sitting back and letting me do the talking. He was a shrewd-looking young buck, though, and I though he'd be a good man to have on our side. I said:

"The woman's going to sue for a settlement and plenty of alimony. Naturally Crandall will get a big fee or a cut on the settlement some way. He isn't working for nothing. That's undoubtedly why they wouldn't let her husband talk to her; they were afraid they'd get the thing straightened out and the divorce idea would be dropped. No divorce; no fee. No fee; no percentage for Crandall. They've probably got that poor gal's head so filled with ideas about her old man that it's spinning."

He said thoughtfully: "You'd think she'd know him well enough not to believe lies about him. That is, if they're lies. Maybe she really has grounds for action."

I said: "Now look! You may know the law but you don't know a hell of a lot about women. They'd rather believe the worst about a man than the best. That's always good. That's true with all of them. They never forget a thing he's ever done, if it's something he shouldn't have done. Their memory isn't so good the other way; they can forget the nice things he's done plenty easy."

He grinned and said: "Hah! A philosopher." I grinned back and said: "Hell no. A guy with experience, God help me."

I told him what had happened, right from the start, and when I got to the place where I'd met the Chief and about the warning the Chief had given me he sat up straight in his chair. He said:

"Lord, man, d'ya realize what this means?"

"Sure," I said. "It means you've got a chief here that knows what it's all about. That's all. Every town is the same. He's playing practical politics, which is something that takes a sense of humor and a strong stomach. He's right; this is a tight little town and he runs it right. A chump in that seat would have this place a mad house in twenty-four hours. Can't you see that?"

"But it means he's working with Crandall."

"It means he's steering a middle course; trying to satisfy Crandall and the other wolves, and trying to do a job for the town at the same time. A bloody reformer in there would raise hell. I tell you; I've seen the same set-up before."

He said he didn't agree and I went on with the yarn. When I came to the place where the man had taken the two pot shots at me he sat up again. He said:

"There's a point right there, Connell. Why would you lose your job right at that time? Why would Crandall try and force the Chief to run you out of town? Why would this attempt be made on your life?"

I laughed and said I guessed somebody didn't like me and didn't want me around.

He said: "It's the time element, man. I'm no detective, but that means something."

"I'm a detective," I said. "And I think you're right. It means something. But I'll be a dirty name if I know what."

I told him what I'd done the night before and about the brawl at the road-house. And about Rucci calling and having me put on the spot. I finished with: "That's how I know Rucci is mixed in the deal some way. That proves it."

"It seems funny to me, Connell, that he'd hire you like that and then fire you. It doesn't seem a reasonable thing to do."

I said: "Well, you've got the picture, now. Suppose you make a date with Crandall and you and I talk with him. As Wendel's lawyer, you're entitled to try and arrange some sort of amicable settlement, at least. Crandall can't refuse that. Maybe we can find out something we can use."

He looked discouraged. "Crandall's too cagy to give out anything he doesn't want us to know, Connell. You might as well know, the man's got one of the finest legal brains I've ever known."

"He's stuck you, hunh?"

He said honestly: "I've never beaten him once. I've tried in seven cases."

"Maybe this will be the time."

"Maybe," he said, and didn't sound hopeful.

He called Crandall's office then and we got an appointment in the next hour. Mard looked a little startled at this action; he acted as though God had condescended to reach down and pat him on the shoulder.

I wasn't startled one bit. I told Mard:

"Hell, guy, I told you there was dough in this case. That fat wolf will talk about dough any hour of the day or night. This kind of dough, anyway."

Mard said he thought I might be right.

Crandall had a honey of an office. Just the best. A dignified young kid bowed at us when we went in, offered to take our hats, and said:

"Mr. Crandall is expecting you gentlemen. I will tell him you're here."

Mard said: "Thank you!"

I said: "And tell the son-of-a-bitch to take that knife out from behind his back. We know him."

The kid looked shocked and left. He came back and led us into a room that matched the reception room for class. Heavy rugs. Big chairs and an Oriental looking affair that was supposed to be a couch. Both the chairs and the couch were decorated with some wild looking covering. Bookcases were recessed into the walls, around three sides, and the fourth looked out on the street. The desk that Crandall sat behind was at least ten feet long and five wide and the top of it looked a foot thick. It was absolutely bare.

The place didn't look like an office, in spite of the bookcases and desk, and it took me a minute to understand why it didn't. It was simple. Instead of law books, with their uniform size and binding, the bookcase section held regular books instead of legal stuff. Crandall saw me eyeing this and grinned at me and said: "That's right, Connell! It's a fake office; just for atmosphere. But I've got a law library as well; Amos here, can tell you that."

I said: "It's swell atmosphere," taking the cue from him. The minute I'd gotten over my mad the night before, I'd been sorry I'd picked him in the Three C Club. Of course he'd made the—trouble for me and knew I knew it, but things like that do no good and sometimes harm. They give bystanders the wrong impression. Amos Mard said: "I'm representing Wendel, Crandall." Crandall raised his eyebrows and looked as though he was enjoying himself. He repeated: "Wendel?" as though it was a question he was asking.

Mard tossed the wire Wendel had sent him in front of Crandall. I'd read it; it only gave Mard authority to represent him. He'd sent another, right along with it, telling Mard to expect me and work with me. I gave Wendel credit for brains on this. Crandall picked up the wire, read it through, and handed it back to Mard. He said, grinning:

"Well that's fine now, Amos. I'm always glad to see a brother in the profession do well. But why do you show this to me?"

"I wanted to talk to you about a settlement. That is, if Mrs. Wendel decides to go through with her action and we decide not to oppose it."

Crandall kept his grin. "Mrs. Wendell isn't a citizen of this state, Amos. She won't be for another month. Naturally she can't sue now. For that matter, she may never sue. She may change her mind; it's a woman's privilege, I've always heard."

Mard started to get red in the face, which was something I'd been afraid of. The trouble with a young man, going up against an old-timer, is that losing temper business and I'd warned him. I broke in with:

"Now look, Crandall. There's no sense or reason in this screwing around. Wendel, naturally, doesn't want his wife to divorce him. That's understood. But if that's what she insists on doing, I don't think he'll fight it. There's no reason for you two to put on this snarling dog business for my benefit. If she divorces him he'll provide for her as a matter of course. Whatever's right. All we'd like to know is what's your idea of right."

Mard turned and frowned at me. After all, he was the lawyer and supposed to be doing the bargaining. But I frowned back and kept on at Crandall with:

"Let's get down to earth on this. What's it going to cost Wendel if it goes through? If it's too steep he'll fight it. He can afford to fight if it will mean a reduced settlement and alimony payments. So let's keep it clean."

Crandall kept that irritating grin. "Now how would I know what Mrs. Wendel wants? What her idea of fair and reasonable is? After all, Wendel is wealthy, or so I understand."

I said to Mard: "He won't talk. Let's go. We're wasting time."

Crandall held up his hand and said: "I just wanted to see if I could take you over the hurdles a bit, Connell. You've got that flary Irish temper and I always enjoy seeing a man lose control of himself. I'll tell you approximately what Mrs. Wendel thinks is fair. Understand, this is tentative; it will bear discussion."

I'd lost my temper and was sore at myself for doing it. He acted on me that way, as he did on Mard. I've always hated the fat, smooth toad type and he was the perfect example. He knew he could drive me crazy mad and gloried in the knowledge and I gritted my teeth and got a bit of control on the ball. I said: "Okey! What's the bad news?"

He said: "She wants to be fair. Wendel is worth, at a conservative estimate, two million dollars. Of course that isn't in cash. We think this kind of settlement would be easy on him; one hundred thousand dollars at once, and fifty thousand dollars a year for three years. This, you will understand, will give Mr. Wendel a chance to raise the money without bleeding his business. And it will make income tax payments easier for Mrs. Wendel. Two hundred and fifty thousand dollars in all. With interest, of course, on the delayed payments."

I said, and tried to keep from choking on the words: "Is that all?" All I wanted to do was get my hands around the fat yegg's throat and be left alone for three minutes.

He grinned back at me and said: "Well, of course that's only the cash settlement. Mrs. Wendel naturally feels she's entitled to alimony as well. But we'll make that a nominal sum."

Mard was as mad as I was. He asked: "Such as?"

"Let us say thirty-six thousand a year. Three thousand a month, though there will be no objection as to how payment is made. Any time convenient with Mr. Wendel will be all right with her I'm sure. She doesn't want to work a hardship on Mr. Wendel; that is why she's asking for such a ridiculously low settlement."

I said: "I think it's mighty white of her to only ask for chicken feed like that. Of course you know and I know that Wendel hasn't two million dollars. What he has is tied up in property. Foreign property and a steamship line and both are nothing that he can take around the corner to Uncle Benny. He can't hock that kind of stuff every day in the week. The guy can't pay anything like that and you know damned well he can't."

Crandall shrugged and grinned. "Well, of course, we can leave it up to the judge. You can trust him to be fair, you know."

"Sure. To Mrs. Wendel."

Mard said: "That isn't fair, Connell. The judge is all right. He'll be fair if he knows the facts."

Crandall made a steeple of his fingers and looked over them at us. "Do you gentlemen know that Mr. Wendel spent three days in our little town a short time ago?"

I said: "Sure. He told me about it."

"Did he tell you what he did?"

"Yes, you bet. He got chased out of town."

"Do you know why?"

"Sure. You put the bee on him."

Crandall shook his head sorrowfully. "That's hardly right. I advised the father of the girl to make no charges. A scandal would only hurt the girl. But he's very bitter about the matter and may change his mind and press the matter. If he does, it will naturally influence the judge. That is only natural. The girl's a Reno girl and the judge has known her all her life. We respect women in this state; I can't understand Wendel's action. You understand, Amos, the position your client is in."

Mard mumbled something and I said: "Cut out the crap, Crandall. What's the frame?"

"Frame!"

"What's this business about a Reno girl and her father?"

He opened his eyes wide, shook his head at me in a pitying way. "I might have known, Connell, you wouldn't have worked for him if you'd known of it. You seem a decent sort. It's merely this. He assaulted a sixteen-year-old girl during the time he was here. Her father, on my advice, didn't press charges. The police rushed him out of town; if the local people had heard of it they possibly would have lynched him. As I said, we respect women in this state."

I said: "Let's go, Mard. This will bear a bit of thinking over."

Mard mumbled something and turned and followed me to the door. Crandall got from behind the desk, came to the door and held it open, then said apologetically:

"I'm sorry about it, Connell, but I thought you knew of the assault. If I'd realized you didn't; that you were here and working for Wendel in good faith, I wouldn't have advised my clients as I did this morning."

"Now what's this?"

"I have three clients. Tony Marsello, Tommy Ryan, and Walter Rans. They happened to be the three men you assaulted last night at the Three C Club. Thinking you were here in an effort to whitewash Wendel on this assault matter, I advised them to file charges against you. Naturally I had no sympathy for you. I'm really sorry about it now."

I said: "This is getting better and better. What charges did they file?"

"Assault with a deadly weapon, I'm afraid."

He was wearing his Cheshire Cat grin and he was just the right distance away. I clipped him on the chin with all I had and he went sailing back and landed all at the same time. Feet, back end, and back of head. He was out colder than any man I ever saw. I said to Mard:

"Well, let's get the hell out of here."

Mard said: "My God, man! They'll hang you for this."

"Nuts!" I said. "He'll probably claim I hit him with a piece of lead pipe, but I've got to expect that in this town. Too much is too much."

We sailed out past his flunkey in the front office and I said: "The mister told me to tell you he wants to be alone. Get it?"

He opened his mouth and gawked and said: "The mister?"

I said: "Yeah! Mr. Bastard!" and jerked my thumb back over my shoulder toward the inside office and Crandall.

CHAPTER TWELVE

Len MacIntosh was waiting for me when I got back to the hotel. Sitting in the lobby and smoking his sissy cigarettes. He climbed up out of his chair, met me, and said:

"Hi there! I've been waiting."

"Long?" I asked.

He shrugged. "A couple of hours, I guess. I've got to take you in."

"Why you?"

"The beef was outside City limits. It's a County case. Get it?"

I said I understood. I turned around and we went outside and started down the street. He said, in a conversational tone: "You know Kirby and I never did like some people in this town, if you know what I mean."

"I've got an idea."

"I've got a notion this charge would be dropped if you left town. It's just a notion of course."

I said: "That'll be the day."

"Well, hell, what can *I* do? I get told what to do, you know that."

"Sure, I know."

"If you'd only keep out of sight," he said, plaintively. "Now if you hadn't just come walking into the lobby like that, I wouldn't have seen you. You make it tough on a man."

I said: "I'm going to make it tough on a man before I leave town. I'll promise you that. If it's the last crying thing I do on this earth I'm going to make it tough on a man. I've run into some cute capers in my life but this one here has got anything beat I ever saw. It's unique. It's so fool-proof there's a hole in it and I'm going to find that hole."

"Why d'ya mean, Connell?"

We were about three blocks up from the hotel by then. I said: "It's this. The bigger and better a frame is, the more people there are in it. The more chance there is somebody forgetting to do or say the right thing. Now there's murder, assault, blackmail, and a few other things in this. Maybe coercion. I know for sure there's another attempted murder in it because I was just about the victim. This beef last night was a frame on me; you know that."

"I work here, Connell!"

"I know it. I don't blame you."

"Kirby and I were talking. D'ya think there's a chance of...
well..." he coughed... "well, your doing anything?"

I said: "I'm getting ideas, if that means anything."

"D'ya think that girl getting knifed ties in with the rest of this?
Kirby does and always has. That's why he's been sort of ... well,
you know."

I said: "Don't say it. I know. You mean you and Kirby can't go
ahead with me unless you're sure you can make it stick. I don't
know that the murder ties in, but everything else has and maybe
that does. I've got the rest of the frame figured but I'll admit the
murder doesn't fit in. I may be wrong on what I think, I'll admit it.
But if I haven't walked into as pretty a frame here as there ever
was, I'm not the picture in it."

He coughed again, said: "Now we're coming to a side street. I
don't suppose I'd happen to notice if you just sort of walked down
it. I can't help it if you escape, can I? But for Christ's sake, tell that
partner of yours to take your baggage down the back way at the
hotel. Everybody ain't reasonable like I am. And when you check
in the Palace Rooms, which is two blocks over and in the middle of
the block, don't tell Maude I sent you. Out loud, that is. And for
Christ's sake keep out of the Three C Club and away from the
police station. There's always phones and I suppose either Kirby or
I could break away from the desk if we had to do it. Now here we
are at the corner."

I said: "What's the name of the cop that took Free and Wendel
to the airport?"

"Ziggy Hunter."

"What kind of a Joe is he?"

MacIntosh spit on the sidewalk and didn't say anything. I said:
"Okey, keed! I'd see that Ziggy took his vacation or something. I've
got to be out on the street sometimes and he's against us."

He nodded and started walking away. His peaked, cocked-up
shoulders were swinging and he was whistling: "When I Leave This
World Behind." It was the first time I'd heard the tune in ten years
or more.

I'd stayed in rooming houses before and for two reasons. Lack
of money for one, and working at the screwy private cop business
for another. But the Palace was a bit different. It wasn't bad and it
wasn't good, but a room there cost as much as you usually pay in

a first-class hotel. And they didn't want their money in advance and that's a rule in all of them. I just said something to the landlady about a man named MacIntosh mentioning the place and I was in with no questions asked about baggage.

This landlady was a hard-looking baggage but she looked smarter than a whip and she proved she was when she looked at me and said with a straight face: "Don't believe I know him. But a lot of people check out after the first night here."

She showed me my cubby hole, said: "The phone's outside in the hall. If you'd like anything to eat, and it's too hot to go out or anything, give me a ring and I'll send out for you. If it's anything I can cook in my own place, I'll do it here. I'm always glad to make an extra dollar."

I said: "This will pay for rent," and gave her a twenty. Then I gave her another one and said: "And this will pay for what I send out for. It'll be used up by the end of the week, of course, but I like to keep ahead."

She said: "Thanks, mister," and clumped away.

There's places like that in a good many towns. If the town is closed for gambling there'll be a big open game running in the upstairs parlor. There's always back and side doors and there will be as many cops in the place as there are hustlers. The cops come in broke and go out with money; the hustlers come in with money and go out broke. A place like that is a necessity. A town is run the way the people want it run, not the way the law says it *should* be run. There has to be a common meeting ground for the law and the outside-the-law crowd, and it's usually some back-street spot that's not too bad and not too good.

A place like that is appreciated. The cops leave it alone and the sporting crowd do the same. They both have to; neither side can afford trouble there. And it's usually run by some smart old gal who knows enough to keep her mouth shut if she should happen to see something she shouldn't. I'd known what I was running into when MacIntosh had cracked about it and I wasn't disappointed. I got outside and to the phone and got Lester... and he was frantic. He said, with his voice trembling so that I could hardly understand him:

"My God, Shean! Where are you? Don't come home. There's a policeman in the lobby waiting to arrest you. He came up here and told me that."

I said: "Okey, kid, I saw him. All he was trying to do was have you go out and find me and keep me away from there. No cop likes to have a prisoner escape on the street in broad daylight."

"What happened, Shean?"

"Nothing much. We've lined up with the cops, is all. That is, some of them. Get my stuff together and bring it to me. Out the back way and to the Palace Rooms. 217. Got it?"

"Well, yes. Are you going to stay there?" I laughed and said I didn't know; that I might be in jail almost any time. Then he said: "What about the car?"

"You'd better bring is over near here. Don't park it by the place, because somebody might see it. Leave it on the next block and remember where, so you can tell me."

"All right, Shean. Right away."

I hung up and went back inside the room and rang the bell for the landlady. She came up and I said:

"D'ya suppose you could get me a quart of whisky?"

"Sure. What kind?"

"Maybe UDL."

I gave her five dollars and she looked at it and said: "Anything you want, mister, is yours. Is there anybody you don't want to see?"

"Hell, yes." She nodded that she understood and turned and went down the stairs. She was back inside of five minutes with the whisky, took a drink with me, then said:

"Now I don't know. But if I didn't want to see any of the bunch that runs around with Rucci, I'd stay in the room when my *buzzer* rang two longs and a short. Understand me, it isn't any of my affair."

I said: "Sure, I know. If I didn't want to run into any of that bunch I'd certainly stay inside."

She hesitated a moment at the door, said: "I've known Len MacIntosh for twenty-two years. I used to have a place in Silver City and he was Marshal there."

"Did he smoke the same kind of cigarettes then?"

She grinned and said: "Yeah! They damned near ran him out because of it. You can't change a man; I've found that out."

Lester came up with my bag and with high blood pressure from excitement. He said: "There were two more cops came, right after you called. One of them was named Ziggy something; I heard the other one call him that."

"That right?"

"Yeah! And Gahagan called and said Wendel had been down at the office. That he said he was coming up here. With Joey Free.

That he was leaving right away."

"How's he coming?"

"She didn't say."

"You get back to the hotel in a hell of a hurry and put in a call and find out. Quick, now."

"And, oh yes, Shean. The girl you were with last night called and wants you to see her right away."

"What about?"

"She didn't say. Just said to call her."

Rucci had introduced me to her and I wasn't sure whether she was planted on me or not. I didn't think so but I didn't know. I said: "Here's her number. You call her back and say you heard from me and that I was leaving town right then. Get it?"

"Sure. Find out how Wendel is coming and tell your girl you've left town."

I said: "You call that wench my girl and I'll beat you black and blue. I may have no morals but, by God, I've got a musical ear."

"I don't understand," he said.

I said: "You either have it or you don't. You haven't, or you'd know what I mean. Now get back and get busy. Just call the place here and ask for 217 and tell me. I'll get in touch with you if I want you; if anything conies up call me here. Get it?"

"Sure!"

"And if you can't get me, get in touch with the Chief. Tell him who you are. He'll know about it, probably. But don't go to the station and don't talk to him on the street. He'll tell you what to do."

Lester looked worried and said: "I don't like this, you having to hide around like this. It's serious."

"You dope! Murder's always serious. I'd rather hide around like this than take a slug in the head, like I almost did. Or end up in the alley like that poor French gal did, with a shiv in my neck. What the hell; d'ya think I like it?"

"Well, no, I guess not."

He took off his glasses and started to polish them, which meant he was thinking hard about something. I said: "Well, get going, pal."

He put them back on, said in a quivery voice: "Shean, if anything happens to you do you know what I'm going to do?"

I said I didn't.

"I'm going to kill Crandall. He's back of this whole thing."

"How would you do it?"

"Well, ugh, I guess I'd shoot him probably. I've practiced, you know that."

He'd tried, down at the shooting galleries, and he'd been pitiful. His glasses didn't help him much and all he had was ambition. I said: "You forget that gun stuff. That's bad medicine. I won't come up missing."

"I'll do it, Shean." I said: "Maybe this will make you feel better. The last I saw Crandall, he was flat on his fanny. He was growing a lump on his jaw that'll be as big as an egg by now. You see?" I showed him the skinned knuckles on my hand and he though that was swell. He told me where he'd left my car, and started back to the hotel, and I took another little snifter of the UDL and thought I'd done better than a green hand on the Crandall job at that. The only way I could have hit him any harder would have been to have been bigger. I only weigh a hundred and ninety and that limits how hard you can sock.

CHAPTER THIRTEEN

There was some connection between the French girl's murder and Crandall and Mrs. Wendel, and I spent the rest of the afternoon trying to figure what it could be. And couldn't. I could see why Crandall would try to keep the woman in the notion of divorce... that was easy. He made money that way; probably some percentage of what he could wangle for her on a settlement. I could see Rucci in the picture as a friend of Crandall's. Undoubtedly, Crandall and Rucci had been together in other deals and Crandall had cut him in this.

But I couldn't see why Rucci had hired me as he had. The firing part was easy; Crandall had spotted me in some way and tipped him off and naturally Rucci didn't want me around the place.

That was another thing. How had Crandall spotted me? The way things had worked out, or rather *hadn't* worked out, it was a cinch that neither Kirby or MacIntosh had spilled any information and somehow I just couldn't imagine the kid had let anything go to his big blonde mama.

Even if he was drunk I didn't think he'd have talked. He was too proud of playing the secretive private detective part. He dramatized himself too much to let slip anything like that, or I was wrong.

But somebody had found out and done the tipping; there was no doubt about that.

The whole thing was screwy and getting no better fast.

I couldn't figure why I'd been shot at when I was. That hadn't been any warning; I still had my sore ear to prove the guy had really tried. It gave me a funny feeling to think that somebody I didn't know was running around the town and trying to see me over the sights of a gun. It was another reason to think the French maid's death was concerned in the Wendel affair in some way. People don't shoot other people over little things. Not that a two hundred and fifty thousand dollar settlement was a little thing, but, after all, Wendel would give his wife the divorce and more than a fair settlement if he was convinced she really wanted it. There was no reason for adding murder to the thing, that I could see.

Crandall had poor Wendel cold, anyway. He'd picked some

little bum, probably some once nice kid that had gone to hell, and fixed a solid rap against Wendel if Wendel bucked at the divorce. It must have been a once nice girl or the judge wouldn't have known her since her childhood. A trick like that would be simple; there's plenty of good kids go wacky when they're still too young to realize what it's all about. I gave Crandall credit; I figured he'd have that part of the frame air tight. He'd take pains with it; he'd have to. It was his ace in the hole, in case Wendel wouldn't go for the divorce settlement.

There wasn't a way in the world I could trace down the girl and try to break her story, either. If it wasn't a frame that would be a cinch; but I had absolutely no way of knowing who he'd pick out to work with on the thing. It probably was some little bum that hung around Rucci's joint, but that didn't help; in the little time I'd worked there I'd seen a dozen that would go for larceny like that.

Crandall was smart enough to bring the frame right from the blue sky if he wanted to use it. It was just a question of keeping him from using it.

For that matter, even if Wendell ever got his wife out of the notion of divorce and took her back to New York, Crandall could still go to town on the assault case and make plenty of trouble. Probably enough trouble to make Wendell pay through the nose to keep it hushed. Wendel was in no position to stand extradition for assault on a sixteen-year-old kid... even if the case wouldn't stand up in court.

And I had the notion Crandall would have it fixed so it *would* stand up.

I got that far with the figuring when Lester called me. He said: "Gahagan said she didn't known how they left. Whether by car, train, or plane. Now what do I do?"

"Wire the plane and the train... both Joey and Wendel. Try both, to make sure they get the page. If they're not on either, it's a chinch they're coming by car. That's probably it; Joey would likely drive it."

"And then what?"

"Then call me back, stupid."

My room door was open and I heard my buzzer signal out two long, then one short ring. I said: "Good-by! Call me later!" and scuttled back in the room and left my door open enough to see who passed by.

First came the big bruiser I'd smacked with the ashtray out at the Three C Club. Then came Kewpie Martin.

The two of them acted very friendly. Kewpie was saying, as he passed my door: "Yeah, I remember one time I got smacked in the puss in St. Paul. Jeese, that guy hit me hard. I remember it was..."

They kept on going down the hall and that was all I heard. The big bruiser's nose was taped and, having had my own schozzle busted once, I knew what they'd done to him. Splinted it up inside so it would heal without leaving too much of a bump.

Kewpie looked his usual fat, cheerful self and not at all like the rat part he was playing. He had his wide grin working good and seemed to be very pally with the lug, and it burned me to think he'd acted the same way with me all the time. I put it down in the debt book about owing him one sweet slam in the face and decided to pay off if, and when, I had the chance.

The two of them were gone not over twenty minutes and they went by in the same order. The bruiser, and then Kewpie. They were both grinning then.

I waited until they were gone, then called Lester and said:

"I was interrupted. Was there anything else? Did you send those wires."

"I sent them. And oh yes. Gahagan said that Joey's check bounced again. She didn't known whether to tell him about it or not, so she let it go. She said you could talk to him about it when you saw him."

"I will."

"And Kewpie came up but that was before I called you before. I forgot to tell you. He asked for you and I said you were out. Should I tell him you've left town?"

I said: "Yeah! And if you can manage to stick around with him, without making him think you're a pest and without him knowing what you're doing, go ahead on it. I'd like to know who he sees and who he doesn't. Try and find out names, if you can do it in a smooth way. Don't come right out and ask; just look interested. He likes to talk and he'll probably tell you by himself."

"Sure, Shean. Why?"

"I'll tell you when I see you," I said, and hung up.

It seemed very likely that Kewpie might know who'd shot at me and might meet him. I didn't know whether finding out who he met would do any good but it couldn't do any harm. It was possible that Kewpie might have been the one that did the shooting. He knew about it and while his story about knowing the news dealer might be all right it might be all wrong.

I had no way of telling and finding a friend in the enemy camp had me bothered plenty. Though I thought there was probably some explanation; Kewpie wasn't the double-crossing type.

Len MacIntosh came up around seven. He knocked once on the door, opened it without waiting for me to do it for him, and came in and said:

"You shouldn't point a gun at a policeman. It makes 'em nervous."

I put my gun down on the dresser and he picked it up and looked at it. He latched the cylinder open, took out a shell, and whistled. He said:

"Christ! I've seen plenty of forty-fives before but I'm damned if I ever saw a load like this. What d'ya call it?"

"It's a hand load. It's a wad-cutter bullet backed with the maximum charge of power. It's got three times the shocking power of the ordinary load or something like that. I forgot just what. But you crease a guy with that slug and it'll knock him down quicker than a smaller slug would if it hit him center."

He put the cartridge back in the gun and closed the cylinder and said: "I can well believe it. You've got the right idea; I never could see any sense in shooting a man more than once. What in hell did you do to Crandall? He was down to the station and I've seen saner people sent a way-to the goofy house. He was crazy; just stark raving crazy."

"What did he do?"

"Nothing. I had to tell him you'd escaped and that you undoubtedly had left town. He couldn't bring you back in the state for simple assault and so he didn't file charges. But if he finds out you're still in town he's going to blow his cork."

I said: "He's going to blow his cork, then. He's going to find out I'm still in town. And if you think he's nuts now, wait until he finds out."

"What you going to do?"

"I don't know," I admitted. "The guy I'm working for is on his way here and I'm going to talk to him first. Now for Christ's sake, tell Kirby not to run him out again until I have a chance to talk to him, anyway."

"I'll tell him. But tell him to keep out of Crandall's sight or it will make it tough for Kirby. You know how it is; Kirby has to live."

"I will."

"Kirby took Ziggy Hunter off regular duty and put him on the desk. He won't see you there."

I said: "I hope not. I don't want to go to the station until this is over. And with him there, it's likely Wendel can stay here for a little while without being recognized."

MacIntosh shook his head. "I don't know. Him and Free ran around the town with no pants on and half the force saw them then. They played around the spots before that and the other half must have seen them there. I don't know. Of course all that will happen will be that he'll be chased out again. Kirby can't afford to do anything else, at this stage of the game."

"He could stay here, couldn't he?"

MacIntosh snorted, said: "Hell, no! It's all right for you; you understand. You're kosher. But that guy! Christ! He'd think he was in a den of thieves and meauw his head off about corrupt police and the rest of that crap. Hell, no, and I don't want you telling him where you are. Nor his friend, this Free. Give me a break."

I said: "I'll tell neither of them, though I can't see the harm in telling Free. He's been around. And I might have to get in touch with him."

"Telling your partner is enough," MacIntosh said positively.

I said: "All right then. I won't."

We talked for a while, just going over things, and he told me Kirby was checking over every sporting man in town that he thought had ever been around New York. In an effort to tie the French girl's murder up with that end of things. He said: "Kirby believes like you do; that there's a connection here with Crandall, but he isn't missing any chances. She doesn't fit in this theory of yours in any way that we can see."

I said: "Listen! You're supposed to be working out of the Sheriff's office, aren't you? You're a deputy. How in hell does it come you and Kirby are so damned chummy? How come you're mixing up with this City stuff? It doesn't make sense."

He said: "Well, I've heard of a man having two jobs at the same time, if you know what I mean. I might even just be on the Sheriff's payroll and not really working for him. But I'm not working for the City; there's no provision for extra help and I couldn't very well go to the council and ask for a job."

I said: "I catch."

He was Government, what branch I didn't know or care. I had the notion he was probably a deputy-marshal but it didn't make the slightest bit of difference. It explained why Kirby had dared to go against Crandall as he had. It meant MacIntosh was after Crandall and that he thought I might be a help to him. It was the answer to a lot of things that had bothered me.

I went on with: "That's swell. That's a break. I want Wendel here when the blow-off comes. I don't want him chased away. If it has to be done, to keep Kirby and Crandall apart, and Crandall still foxed, let Kirby run him out and you go with him and see he's brought back."

"Wendel will have to be here, you think?"

"I don't think; I know. We've got to have him."

"Why?"

MacIntosh had cold grey eyes, set under damned near white eyebrows. The eyebrows were bushy and needed plucking badly. They were mean eyes and he turned them on me and waited for an answer and all I could say was:

"I'm not sure yet. I can't crack until I've got more to go on. If I'm right in what I think, he's got to be here."

"Why not spill what you think?"

"I've got nothing to go on. Just a notion."

"Is the French girl mixed in it?"

"She must be. I'm not sure just how."

"Both Kirby and I have given you every break, Connell. Why not play back?"

I said: "Damn it! I can't tell you something I don't know. I've missed something and I'm trying to figure what it is. I can't get it. Why should somebody try to kill me like that? There's only one answer; I've stumbled into something and haven't brains enough to see it. It'll come to me. The French girl is mixed in it someway but I don't know how. She don't fit in the picture anyway. A murder throws things wide open and this bunch is smart enough to know it. They'd never have done it unless it was forced on them. What forced it? What made them panicky? When I know I've got the answer to the whole thing."

"Suppose I get help and you and I and Wendel demand to see his wife? Would that bring the showdown?"

"How would it? He'd never get a chance to talk sense to her like that. She'd go ahead and get her damned divorce, which is just what Crandall wants. What are you after him for?"

I rang that last in quick, thinking I could possibly stampede him into telling me something. He just grinned, said: "That's a sort of secret, Connell. But I'll tell you this; Rucci is mixed in it too."

"It's either white-slave stuff or dope."

"You've got a right to guess. I can't stop you guessing." I said: "Let's call it a draw. I can't tell you anything and you won't tell me anything. Let me talk to Wendell and work something out."

He stared at me a moment, said: "I want to be in at the finish, guy. I'll talk to Kirby."

He left, and left me staring at the four blank walls, trying to figure the connection between the murdered French girl, the attempt to kill me, and Mrs. Wendel's refusal to talk with her husband.

And trying to tie Kewpie and the rest of the complications in with the mess in general. None of it made sense.

CHAPTER FOURTEEN

I went out that night and met Lester and his blonde mama, then went over and took the Spanish looking girl for a ride. I didn't think she was mixed up with Rucci and it was so damned monotonous sitting in the room that I thought I'd go crazy. I told her: "Do me a favor, hon, and don't say anything about seeing me."

She said: "Why? Are you ashamed of me?" I said I wasn't. She had brains enough to know I was in some kind of jam with enough extra not to ask about what it was. If it hadn't been for her voice she'd have been a swell kid. It was just another count against the music business; If I hadn't been in that so long I probably would never even thought of how she talked. I got back to the Palace Rooms late and slept the same way the next morning. Lester woke me by calling about ten and what he said brought me wide awake. He said:

"Mr. Wendel and Joey are here. They want to see you."

"There in the room?"

"Oh no. They checked in the hotel. They're cleaning up now."

"The damned fools! Don't they know the cops will run them out if they see them?"

"Joey's drunk again, Shean! He told me he has his false whiskers along and that he's going under a disguise. He's going to be the old man of the mountain he says."

"Oh Christ," I said. "What are they registered under? What names? Is Wendel drunk?"

"Wendel's sober. They're registered under the names of O. M. Mountain and Dick Smith."

I wanted to laugh but I was too mad to do it. Wendel, the poor innocent, wouldn't know that Dick Smith was a gag name, and Joey Free's O. M. Mountain business had me wacky. I wouldn't have put it past the screwball to don a long white beard and go down to the station and ask if they'd heard of a Mr. Joey Free lately. He was that dizzy when drunk. I said to Lester:

"They'll see you again, I'm afraid. Tell Wendel I want to see him. But don't call this number when he or Joey are in the room and don't tell them where I am. This is a secret, kid, I told you that."

"I know, Shean!"

"Did Joey say anything about his rubber check?"

"He took me to the side and gave me the hundred to give to you. I told him you were in trouble and that I met you now and then, where you told me to. Was that right?"

"Sure. Now listen. If Joey's drunk, keep it just with Wendel. Tell him to meet me at the corner of Virginia and K streets at nine tonight. Of course if Joey is sober, it's okey to tell him too. The only thing is, I don't want Joey around if he's drinking. I'm hotter than a forty-five right now and he'd make it that much tougher. Understand?"

"Sure, Shean! Can I come too?"

I thought and couldn't see what harm it would do. I wasn't planning on doing anything but picking up Wendel in the car and driving out of town a bit and telling him what had happened. I had an idea how boring it must be for Lester; staying in the room just the time I had was driving me dizzy:. So I said: "Sure."

I went back in the room and put the rest of my clothes on and asked the landlady to bring me something for breakfast. She did and handed me an envelope along with it, and I opened this and found a gun permit and a note from MacIntosh. The note read: "Connell—I got the number of that cannon of yours yesterday and thought you might want a permit for it. You need one for this state. Your California permit and license are no good here. It won't be traced and I signed for you. MacIntosh."

The permit was issued by a J. P., a few miles out of town and it had my gun number right. It was a help; it gave me a legal right to carry the gun and God knows I thought I might need it. I was having more respect for Len MacIntosh every day I knew him. The landlady took pity on me that afternoon and came up and we played coon-can for four bits a game and a dollar a tab and she took me for fourteen bucks but it was worth the price of admission. She told me yarns about the Nevada of the old days; she was sixty-two, although she didn't look over fifty, and she'd lived in the state since she was sixteen. She'd done everything and that was truth. She'd been shot three times and stabbed once; brawls in places she'd ran. She knew all the old-timers who're history now... and the things she knew about them weren't the history that's common knowledge. She'd been through gold and silver rushes... she'd been in the money herself twice over, grub-staking prospectors... and here she was running this place. She wasn't in the least bitter about losing her money... part of it had gone in bad mining ventures and part in the last stock market crash... and she said:

"Why should I squawk? I had fun with it. I made it and I spent it. Why cry about it?"

I said: "Most women don't feel that way."

She said: "I've lost more money playing high low Jack than most women have ever held in their hands. What good is it; you can't eat it, can you? It won't cover you when you're cold."

"It will buy what it takes, won't it?"

She grinned and said: "Hell! You can only eat one meal at a time and sleep in one bed. It's nothing to worship."

I thought that if Crandall had the same notion, Wendel would maybe have been spared a lot of grief.

I stalled until nine and then drove around to the corner where I was to meet Wendell. He and Lester were waiting on the corner and I pulled into the curb and said:

"Climb in."

They did, with Wendel in the middle. He started to cry before I'd even gotten the car away from the curb. He said:

"I'll say now, Connell, that I'm disappointed in you. Free told me you were a good man but I think you've mismanaged this affair most lamentably."

"Did you do better?" I asked.

He admitted he hadn't.

"I walk in here on a set-up that's damned near perfect and you expect me to crack it. I've got the whole damned town against me and you expect me to perform a miracle."

"I can't understand your antagonizing the police the way you have. I can't understand that at all."

"They haven't put me on any plane, mister."

"I don't understand your idea in taking a position in that roadhouse. Your friend told me of that."

"I met your wife there."

He shut up for a moment, said in an altered voice: "How... how did she look?"

"Okey, as far as I could see."

"Who was she with?"

"Her lawyer."

"No one else?"

I couldn't see any sense in telling him she'd been with her lawyer as well as two hoodlums and their tramp women. But I knew what he was thinking of and I said:

"Now look! I thought the same as you're thinking when I started out on this. I figured boy friend, the same as you do. But

I've seen her several times, twice out there, and she's always been with either her guards or her lawyer. And the lawyer's no boy friend of hers. So get that out of your craw. It's something else. Now did you meet any sixteen-year-old kids while you and Joey were painting the town?" He stared at me. We were parked by that time and I could watch his face. He said: "Why of course not. We were in bars and gambling places. Naturally I didn't meet any children in those sort of places."

"They start young sometimes. A gal can fool you on age. Put it this way; were you out with any woman?"

He said stiffly: "I was not. I was here to effect a reconciliation with my wife. Naturally I would not be with any other woman. That sort of casual affair doesn't appeal to me, anyway. Even before my marriage."

I said: "You know it's statutory rape if the girl's under sixteen. Even if she's willing. You've got that straight? Don't lie to me, Wendel, I've got to know."

He looked at me as though I was crazy and said: "1 haven't the faintest idea of what you're talking about. Please explain."

I said: "I thought it was a frame but I had to make sure." I went on and told him of what Crandall had said and his face got redder and redder and he swore in a school-boyish way. But very sincerely. I kept on with the explaining, showing him the spot he was on. I finished with:

"Now get it. If you contest the suit, Crandall will get this father of the girl, whoever she is, to swear out a warrant charging you with this mythical assault. You'll be picked up on the charge at once, if you're in the state. They could extradite you on it, if they wanted to, but I doubt if they would. They'll be satisfied to have you away. If you fight it, the judge has got two strikes called on you before you open your mouth; Crandall tells me the judge knows the girl they've got working with them. Of course the judge thinks she's a sweet innocent kid. You're going to get stuck with that robbing settlement if the thing goes through. There's no way out of it."

"But... but won't my wife's action come up long before any criminal charge could be brought against me and carried to trial?"

"Not in this town. I don't say Crandall can influence the judge; I don't think he can. But he sure as hell can get a criminal case speeded up if he wants to pull a few strings. Christ, man! I guess you don't realize the influence a man like that carries in this sort of town. Look at it this way. He's in with the decent people and he's in with the crooks. Suppose some reputable person makes a slip.

Crandall has his underworld element to tell him of the slip, as well
as his decent friends and the things he learns through his own
practice. He's got people like that foul; they'll jump when he
speaks. He's been here for years. A situation like that snowballs;
I'm willing to bet he knows as much about the private life of this
town as the town does. He can bring pressure to bear in a
thousand different ways. It's a form of blackmail; but he keeps in
the clear all the time."

"But this is a pure and simple frame-up."

Lester made one of the few wise remarks I ever heard him
make. He said gravely: "Pure frame-up perhaps, but surely not a
simple one. It seems very complicated to me."

Wendell ignored him, said to me: "Isn't there anything I can
do?"

"D'ya think you can straighten this if you can talk with your
wife?"

"I can try at least. I don't understand her action; I've done
nothing to warrant it. If I can talk with her I think I can convince
her of that."

He looked down on the floor-board then, said in a sick sort of
way: "I'll tell you, Connell. If she really wants to divorce me I won't
stand in her way. I'll give her any settlement she asks for if it's
possible for me to do it. But there's a mistake here; there must be."

"D'ya want this blood-sucker of a Crandall to get the
settlement she's asking for? I'm telling you; the man isn't in it like
this for a straight fee. That doesn't make sense. There's big money
in it for him or he wouldn't be fooling around. Hell, man, there's a
murder in it. Why I don't know, but there's a tie-up. Would a
supposedly reputable lawyer fool with murder for a divorce case
fee? Use your head on this. I'm not bucking your wife's settlement.
You're not. It's Crandall; he's back of it."

"I know all that. Why tell me that?"

"I don't want you going soft on me."

He put his dignified air back on and said: "My personal
feelings are, after all, my own affair and concern."

I cracked it at him then. I'd been wanting to do it all the time,
but he was such a straight-laced bird I'd been afraid to speak. I
said: "It's my concern if it puts my neck in a noose. Don't forget
that, mister. Now if you want to take a chance, we'll try and talk
with your wife."

"Where can we see her?"

"At Crandall's place."

He looked bewildered, stuttered: "B-b-ut the guards! I tried to speak with her before. I've told you that."

I laughed and said: "We're going in the side way or the back way or some way where the guards aren't. I don't know just how and won't, until I case the house. But we'll try it if you've got the guts."

He said very simply: "I want to see her."

CHAPTER FIFTEEN

The three of us drove out to the Three C Club and I parked in the shadow beyond it and sent Lester in to see what he could see. He came out, giggling, and said:

"She's in there with Crandall and the two guards. And Joey's there."

"Drunk?"

"Very. He's at the bar, sitting on the edge of it. He's got a Santa Claus beard on and he's singing Coming Round the Mountain. And telling everybody that the song is written about his mountain."

This was a new high, even for Joey. I said: "Did you see Rucci?"

"He was trying to get Joey to climb down from the bar. Joey's got a lot of money, though, and I guess Mr. Rucci doesn't want to make him mad so he'll go someplace else. Every now and then Joey shouts 'Fire in the head' and everybody goes to the bar and has a drink. Joey pays for them."

This was enough to get Wendel's mind off his troubles, even if only temporarily. He asked curiously:

"What does 'Fire in the head' mean?"

"That's a term hard rock miners use," I said. "They put powder in the face of the cutting. I mean, down in the shaft they're drilling."

He looked bewildered and I explained: "They tunnel a shaft into the rock. Then they bore holes in the face of it and fill them with powder or dynamite. Then they light the fuses on these shots and yell 'Fire in the head' and everybody in the shaft runs like hell so they'll be away when the explosion comes. Do you see now?"

He said: "Frankly, I don't. Possibly I'm stupid."

I didn't give him any argument on the last. I said: "Well, when somebody shouts 'Fire in the head' in a bar, everybody in the place runs up to get a drink. It's free, you see. Some wit saw the rush and thought of the mining term ... or maybe it was the other way around. Anyway, it's an old saying and everybody out here knows what it means."

Lester said: "That's very interesting," and Wendel said: "I'm afraid I have no sense of humor."

I said nothing; there was no proper answer.

We cruised around until twelve, then went to a hole in the wall and ate. I called the station and tried to get Kirby, but he'd gone home. I tried the Sheriff's office for MacIntosh and got the same answer. It didn't make a great deal of difference; I just wanted to call in so they'd know things were moving along. I had no intention of telling them the plan I'd made for Wendell and myself.

We went back to the Three C then and Lester went in and out and reported that Joey was bogged down in a booth, with Rucci and two men he hadn't seen before. That Joey was drunk but no drunker. I said: "Hell! That man can't get any drunker. There's such a thing as a saturation point." And then, because thinking I'd seen Joey drive by me there in Reno still bothered me, I asked Wendel: Did you tell me Joey went to Los Angeles?"

"Why yes. He called me at least once a day from there. I judged he wasn't drinking, either."

Lester said the Wendel party showed signs of leaving so we drove back and past where Crandall lived. I parked in the shadow beyond the house and well away from it, and I said to Lester: "Now you sit here in the car and blow the horn if a police car comes by and stops. Then get out and run like hell. Not down the street; take off across lots. They can't catch you then as easily."

"Why can't I come with you, Shean?"

"I'm going to have trouble enough looking after myself and Mr. Wendel, and I can't take the extra chances, kid." I realized how this would make him feel and switched the meaning with: "I can't take chances with a bunch of cops stopping our get-away. You've got to stay here and give me warning."

He said seriously: "Oh yes! The lookout man. Should I blow the horn in any sequence?"

I didn't get it. I repeated "sequence" and he said: "Why of course. You know. Like four times or three times. For the signal, you know."

I said: "Say three times. Then run." I didn't have any idea of police coming but I didn't want the kid tagging along and tripping over his shoe laces. He was blind as a bat in day time and at night he's even worse. I'd have had to lead him by the hand, as though he were a little child.

A big sedan came down the street and turned into the Crandall drive and stopped in front of the door. We watched more lights flick on, all over the house and I said:

"Now I'm going to do some guessing. It's a cinch the bedrooms will be on the second floor. The best, which would be the master's bedroom, will be in the front. There's two bedrooms in the front and that will mean that your wife, who's the honored guest, will have one and our Mr. Crandall will have the second. How's that for reasoning?" Wendel said: "It seems logical."

Lester said: "But which is the first and which is the second?

"That's elementary. Mrs. Wendel is a guest. She'll naturally go to bed first, because Crandall will wander around and see that everything's okey before he tucks in. In common politeness he'd stay up until she went to bed. Simple?"

Lester said, with admiration: "That's pure deduction."

Wendell said: "Humph!"

The upstairs light on the left of the house snapped on-first. We watched it. Ten minutes afterward it went out. A few minutes later the right hand one went on in turn. We watched that. In five minutes it went out. I said: "Check and double check. Mrs. Wendel would put cold cream on her face to take off the make-up. That would take a little while. Crandall would just take off his clothes and pile in bed. It proves my theory."

I was just guessing but it sounded reasonable, even to myself. And Lester thought I was the second Sherlock Holmes and I didn't want to disappoint him. God knows I hadn't shown any brilliance in the case up to that time and I thought he was entitled to something that would back up his blind faith. I looked at Wendel in what little light the dash lamp gave and his face looked drawn and worried but he didn't seem afraid. I said:

"Now look, mister. You're not going to crack up on me in there, are you? I'm going first and see that everything's clear, but I want you right behind me. I don't want to look for you and find you where you don't belong."

He smiled a little, said: "I want to see my wife. I'd do worse than this, Mr. Connell. Don't worry."

Lester asked: "What are you going to do about the guards?"

"They'll probably be in bed. If one of them sits up it'll be in front. We'll wait; we can tell by the lights."

There was a light in the front room but it was turned off about then. I said: "The chances are somebody sleeps in the front room on a couch or something. Or maybe the two bozos just took a last drink. It doesn't make any difference; we're not going in through the front."

The house was dark and I looked at my watch and said: "In half an hour," and opened the glove compartment and took out a bottle. I passed it to Wendel and he shook his head... and I took his share. The more I thought of this house-breaking idea the screwier it seemed to me. My feet were getting colder than Wendel's must have been.

The half hour finally passed and it didn't seem like more than six. Waiting for something when you're afraid makes time drag. But the time came and I climbed out and said: "Come on," to Wendel.

He followed me and I told Lester to remember what he was to do and led the way toward the house. As soon as we got where Lester couldn't hear me I kept my voice low and said to Wendel:

"Now listen and for Christ's sake remember it. If there's action it's likely to come in a bunch. If anybody shoots at us, you drop down on your face and get as close to the floor as you can. Don't move, no matter what happens. Even if you think you can get away. The worst that can happen to you, if you're caught, is that you'll be put in jail. But if you run, you're liable to get a bullet in the back and they don't set bail on that."

He said he understood and that he'd do it. "And if anything like that happens don't pay any attention to me. I may run; I may not. I don't know. You just drop flat and let the thing go on."

He said impatiently: "I understand, Connell. You don't have to repeat yourself."

"Did you ever have anybody shoot at you?"

"Of course not."

"Well, I have. It's easy to forget things at a time like that, mister. We'll try it at the sides, first."

I could see his face, there was enough light for that, and I could see he was a bit whiter but looked as though he was going through with it. It's tough, running into a thing like that, and he had brains enough to know it. The guards were certainly armed and probably Crandall would have a gun in his room. And his wife's room and Crandall's were almost next door; probably only a hall between them.

At that, he wasn't any more afraid than I was. He couldn't have been. I didn't have any wife to take my mind off the danger.

We pussy-footed up to the side of the house and I started to try windows. This after taking off our shoes. I didn't think Crandall would have anything like burglar alarms on the windows; damned few private houses have, and this didn't worry me. But the thought of a squeaky window did.

They all were locked... both sides. We went to the back of the house, tip-toed up on a broad back porch and tried the back door and found it the same way. I tried the three pass keys I had and no dice. Then Wendel gripped my arm, pointed down the porch, and hissed: "That window's open."

It was... and it was a mortal cinch it was a back bed-bedroom and belonged either to some of the house help or the guards. I went to it, peeked in and could see a shadowy outline of a bed and could hear somebody wheezing. It wasn't a snore and from the sound of it I couldn't tell whether it was a man or woman. I took my sap out of my back pocket and whispered to Wendel: "Let me get by the bed. Then you come in. For Christ's sake be careful."

He squeezed my arm to show me he understood.

I climbed through the window, trying to keep my clothes from rubbing on the sill and making a noise, and got inside with no yowl coming from the bed. I knelt down by it so I could get the sleeper's face outlined against the wall, and saw it was a woman. I got ready to shove her pillow in her face, if she woke, and Wendel started to come in.

I'll give him credit. He had the instincts of a first class second-story worker. The guy must have been a thief at heart. He came through the window like a ghost.

We slipped through the bedroom door, which made one squeak when I opened it, and saw a hall leading toward the front of the house and an open door to the kitchen. I whispered to Wendel:

"There's probably back stairs but we can't look for them. We'd be bound to tack into something that would rattle. Keep about ten feet back of me but keep coming."

He squeezed my arm again.

I went down the hall and it jogged, right by the front door, showing a staircase going up. There was a door leading to a front room on each side and from the left I could hear good hearty husky snores and I never heard better music in my life. I went up the stairs, walking close to the wall as I'd told Wendel to do, in order to lessen the chance of a squeaky tread, but the house was old and warped and those damned stairs sounded as loud to me as any brass band I ever heard.

But not a sound, outside of that.

I got to the top and waited for Wendel, and I could hear him coming all the way. Not alone from the stairs but because of his breathing. He was wheezing like he had asthma. I whispered to him when he got to me: "For God's sake breathe slower."

He whispered back: "I'll try."

The tough part was coming. What we'd done was kid stuff, compared to waking his wife up and keeping her from waking up the household. I said:

"What pet name did you have for her?" He grunted, made a rattling noise in his throat that sounded like: "E-r-r-r," and didn't say anything.

"You must have called her something besides Ruth." He whispered: "I-I-I called her p-puzzums." I said: "Oh Jesus!" and wanted to laugh in spite of the spot I was on, but I said instead: "Now when we get inside you get you face close to her ear and be ready to whisper in it. Then just put your hand over her mouth and whisper. For Christ's sake, don't let her make that first squawk. She'll come out of her sleep scared to death and she'll sing out sure as hell. So clamp down on her mouth until she knows who it is that's talking to her. Understand." He said he did.

I went down the hall and got to her door and tried it. It was unlocked, and if I'd been a gal in that den of wolves that door would have been bolted and propped closed with a chair as well. But I thanked God for her trust in men and opened it.

I took plenty of time doing it; at least five minutes. And Wendel was at the back of my neck, breathing like a fire horse after a run. I finally got it cracked enough for us to lip through and I went first, to make sure my Sherlock Holmes stunt had been right.

It had been. It was a warm night; the front windows were open and letting in quite a bit of light, and the gal had kicked off the covers. I couldn't make a mistake; there was no doubt of it being Mrs. Wendel. I slipped to the other side of the bed, where I could help hold her if she came out of her corner fighting, and Wendel knelt down by her.

Her nightie was thin and not exactly where it belonged and knowing Wendel for such a Puritan I felt sorry for him. After all, a man and his wife should have secrets and she'd given hers away. I'd have been willing to bet his face was red and I wouldn't have taken the short end gambling that mine wasn't.

He put his hand over her mouth, ready to grab, got his face close to the side of her head, then reached over with his other hand and patted her cheeks.

And clamped down over her mouth.

She came out of it all in a bunch. She bridged herself like a wrestler trying to break a hold and started kicking. I'll give him credit. He hung on, now with both hands, but it was a grasp of desperation. His mind had given away under the strain and he was whispering hoarsely: "Puzzums! Puzzums! Puzzums!" over and over again.

I got one hand over his, on her mouth, and leaned across her, trying to hold her so she couldn't get free. She was bucking like a horse. Finally he quieted down and I took my hand away, and he got himself together and said:

"This is Tod, honey. I've got to talk to you."

She kept quiet. He repeated his identification and added: "It's all right, honey. We won't hurt you; we just want to talk to you. Now will you whisper and not make any noise?"

Then he said: *"Arrrgghh!"* and it was no whisper. It was damned near a shout. Instead of trying to hold his hand over her mouth he tried to take it away, and she came right up with it, holding it with her teeth. She was shaking her head like a damned dog and she was screaming at the top of a plenty husky voice.

If I'd been him she'd never have sued for a divorce; she'd never have been able to sue or do anything else in this world. I'd rather have a wild tiger in the house than a woman who bites. I'd have lowered the boom. But he just jerked away and said: *"RUTH!"*

She went off that bed like a wildcat and she kept yowling like one. I said to the dope: "Come on! Quick!"

I led the way into the hall and there she was, pounding on the door of Crandall's room and making the night hideous with her voice. Wendel ran to her, took her by the shoulder, and said again: *"RUTH!"*

She turned and caught him fair in the nose with her fist and I could hear the good solid sound it made when it landed. He took a couple of steps back toward me and I grabbed him and pitched him toward the stairs and said: "Get going fast."

He did... with me following. We went down the stairs, sounding like a herd of horses, and just when we got to the foot of them the lights snapped on and a guy said: "Hold it!"

It was one of the plug-uglies I'd met at the Three C Club. He was dressed in undershirt and shorts and a .45 Colts Automatic and the last impressed me because it pointed at me, where I stood above Wendel. The Wendel woman's screams above stopped short, and then Crandall's voice came from the head of the stairs saying: "Hold them, Barney!" Barney grinned and said: "Yeah!" The other guard came out of the door behind Barney and this one was dressed in just shorts. He had a mat of hair on his chest and looked absolutely indecent and he held a gun against his hip bone but so it pointed toward us. He asked Barney: "Everything under control?"

Barney jerked his head and said: "Yeah!" again. Crandall called down: "Tell 'em to turn around so I can see who it is. I can guess now."

Wendel turned and I could see blood pouring from his nose. I turned also, and Crandall said: "Hagh! I was right. Hold them, Barney, and I'll call the police." Barney said: "Yeah!"

Crandall was wearing about the loudest suit of pajamas I ever hope to see in this world. Purple and red. He looked like a big fat toad in them. He said to me: "You should have stayed out of town, Connell. You'll do time for this."

I said: "Call the cops and shut your God-damned mouth."

Barney said: "Turn around!" and then: "Now come down here and face the wall."

He waved the gun toward the wall opposite him, and Wendel and I did what we were told to do. Barney's gun waving didn't take the muzzle a hell of a way out of line and there was the partner, behind him, to back him up.

It was no time for heroics.

He took my gun and sap and fanned Wendel, who was clean. He hefted my gun, which weighs forty-four ounces when empty, then slammed it against the side of my head. I rolled with the blow, taking away quite a bit of the punch, but it put me down to my knees. Wendel said:

"Here! Here! That's not necessary."

He sounded calm and cool then. The shock of getting nabbed had straightened him instead of doing the other. Barney said: "You want some of it too, eh?"

"That isn't necessary."

Barney made a half-hearted cut at him with my gun, missing him a foot, intentionally. I stayed on my knees, shaking my head to clear it, and Wendel asked: "Are you hurt?"

I managed to stand up and said: "No. But when I get that bastard with no percentage he's going to be."

Barney laughed and said: "Yeah!"

Crandall called down: "I've called the station and they're sending over. Just hold them, men."

I turned my head and could see Wendel's wife standing by Crandall. Wendel was already looking up at her; not saying anything. She saw us and ducked back out of sight and Wendel said to me under his breath:

"I'm getting over it, Connell."

I said: "Well, it's time."

And then we waited for the wagon.

There were four men in it and Barney, the guard, started out with calling the one in charge: "Ziggy!" He said: "Ziggy, these two birds busted in and we got 'em dead to rights. The old man will charge 'em with everything in the book."

"Where is he?" this Ziggy asked. He was a big burly red-faced man and he'd have won in a beauty contest. The consolation prize.

"Up dressing. You got here quick."

"I'm on the desk."

He swung on me and said: "So you're Connell, eh?"

I nodded.

"You're the guy that's been raising so much hell? Start something now, why don't you?"

I said: "You loud-mouthed son-of-a-bitch! Take off that badge and gun and I will. I'm willing to bet your pals would like to see you take it, too."

Two of the cops grinned and the other said: "That's resisting an officer, Ziggy. That's another charge."

I said to him: "Another—, hunh?"

The first two cops kept their grins. I was getting a break; two against two. Even-Stephen. The cop got red and mumbled something and I said: "Spit it out, baby. Take off the jewelry and I'll take you on after Mister bastard here."

Crandall said, from the stairs: "Quite a guy, eh, Connell? You know an officer can't brawl like that. I wouldn't blame either of these men if they subdued you by force after that. I think it would be justifiable."

Ziggy came out with a sap. So did his pal. One of the other cops said: "Hey, Ziggy. Now there's no need of..." Ziggy cut at me with the sap then and I dodged it. The dodge took me in the other one's range and I didn't do as good there. The sap caught me across the ear and made me wobbly. Wobbly enough to let Ziggy catch me fair and square with his next try.

I came back to life in the wagon and the wagon was stopped in front of the jail. The wagon was only a five passenger sedan but they're all the same, whether they've got wire over the back of a truck or are just an ordinary car. They all take you to jail. I could hear Ziggy's voice say:

"Get 'em out," and then I heard Kirby's voice drawl: "And what is this, Hunter?"

"Two guys charged with house-breaking, assault, and a bunch

of other stuff. Connell is going to face a gun charge. The other guy is going up against aggravated assault. Crandall is coming down to charge them."

Kirby said: "Just a minute. Aren't you supposed to be on the desk?"

"Wilson's taking my place."

"Did I put you on the desk or Wilson?"

"Well, you put me."

"Why aren't you there?"

"Well ... I ..."

Kirby laughed but it didn't sound funny. He said: "Somebody else is running the force, is that it? You get inside where you belong and you do it God-damned fast."

I could hear his feet clumping away and then Wendel climbed out. I followed him and had a hard time making it; Ziggy's sap hadn't helped me much. Kirby said to the cops:

"We'll take charge of these men. I want to talk with them."

He led the way, with MacIntosh following Wendel and me. We went in the office and Kirby sat us down and said to me: "What crack-brained stunt is this, Connell?"

The wallop hadn't helped me think, either. I said: Well, Wendel wanted to see his wife. So we went to see her."

MacIntosh grinned and said to Kirby: "There's no charges filed against them, that I can see. Of course there's that old charge against Connell but that's County and I haven't any memory tonight. I don't see how you can hold them."

The brain worked better then. I said: "Suppose you hold Mr. Wendel tonight and let me out. That's splitting the difference."

Wendel said: "I don't understand, Connell."

"You're safe in jail. I'm not. Not with this Ziggy loose."

Kirby got red and said: "That wasn't my fault. I thought I had him out of the way."

"His Master's voice," I said. "Crandall's."

MacIntosh stared at me and said: "Then you want out and Wendel wants in. That it?" I nodded.

Wendell said: "Connell, this is ridiculous. I demand that I be allowed to see a lawyer and have a hearing and bail set. I don't want to spend any time in jail."

He looked away from me and at Kirby and I shook my head at MacIntosh. MacIntosh stood and said: "After all Connell knows what he's doing, Mr. Wendel. Or he's supposed to know. Suppose you let him play it his way."

Wendel said indignantly: "Now Connell, I won't stand for this. I won't put up with it."

MacIntosh nodded at me and then toward the door and I got up and said to Wendel: "Now look! I don't want to be tied down and have it known where I'm tied. It doesn't matter about you; they won't shoot at you in jail. I don't think Crandall will put charges against you and I know damn' well he will against me."

He argued: "We both did the same thing."

"They're afraid of me and they're not of you. It makes it different. And I want to try out something. I want to see if charges are filed against you, if you want to know."

He shook his head, made a motion with one hand and grumbled: "Well, all right. I think it's a silly thing to do."

"If it wasn't for me the police would hold you anyway, so what's the difference?"

He nodded then, said: "Well, all right." I said: "I'll see you soon," and went out in the hall. MacIntosh followed me out and said: "It's your play, Connell, but it doesn't make sense to me. You're safer in jail than out."

"I could be followed when I got out; now I can make my sneak. I'll be back at the Palace if you want me."

"There's going to be hell to pay for this tomorrow. You know that."

"I want Wendel where he's safe. That's all. I want him where I can get him if I need him. It may be I'll want him in a hurry. If he gets out and runs into Joey Free, God knows where he'll be. With Joey drunk like he is, he's liable to start for either Mexico or Canada; he does things like that."

MacIntosh grinned. "He's a wild Indian; I know that. Kirby says he's a good egg. But wild."

I said: "He's the old man of the mountains, that's all."

And left for the Palace Rooms.

CHAPTER SIXTEEN

I called Lester as soon as I got to the phone and he was jittery. He'd stuck around the house and saw us leave with the police escort and it had him worried sick. I said: "Never mind that. Get a cab and go out to the Three C Club and get hold of Joey Free. That is, if he's not in his room. Get him sober. It'll be a job but you do it. I'm going to need him in the morning. Get it?"

"Yes, Shean! But what if I can't get him sober?"

"Get him in shape to dig up some dough. That's all I ask. Wendel is going to want bail money and I don't want to get in touch with New York for it. Joey can dig it up in less time. This is going to break damned soon."

Lester said, in a bewildered way: "But why will it break soon, Shean? She can't sue for divorce until she's been here six weeks, can she? She hasn't been here for over three, now."

I said: "I can't tell you over the phone, kid. Get out and get Joey and get him right. Crandall's going to get action; he's going to figure out a settlement with Wendel right soon and Wendel's sick enough about the business to go for it. And a widow's share in the estate will run into money too. Think it over."

I hung up then and let him think it over. I hadn't told Wendel, because there was no reason to worry him, but I was starting to think he had no business running around loose. I didn't know the New York law, but it seemed reasonable to suppose a widow would get a hefty share of what estate he'd leave ... if she suddenly became a widow, that is. And I wasn't under any illusions about Crandall... I figured he'd make Mrs. Wendel a widow and think nothing of it if it paid him to do it.

But I didn't think I could make Wendel see this argument. There was nothing I could prove as yet. There was nothing to do but protect him, as well as myself, and let things come to a head.

She'd been in town about half her time; the opposition had still three weeks to do their business. There'd been one murder in the forty-two days they had to work in ... and I didn't want to be the star in another. Or for my client to be starred. I wanted Joey to have bail all ready to put up so that I could get Wendel out of town if it seemed advisable.

Crandall had missed a bet when he hadn't done a lot of

shooting there in his house. The action came so fast he didn't have a chance to study the angles. If he'd shot then he'd have been in the clear, being able to prove we'd broken in and all. He'd have been justified in thinking us burglars and acting accordingly. He'd think of that golden opportunity he'd missed, that I knew, and he wouldn't overlook another chance.

And I didn't want Wendel running around the streets with Joey Free and giving Crandall that break again.

Lester called me in the morning and said: "I've got Joey and he's in pretty good shape. He sobered up quickly."

"He's had a lot of practice," I said. "Where'd you find him?"

"At the Three C. He was still thinking he was the old man of the mountain but when I told him what had happened he sobered up."

"Where is he now?"

"Here with me."

I couldn't go to the hotel and talk with him and Lester had my car. I couldn't remember the name of any bar in town, except the Rustic, and I didn't want to go there because of Gino Rucci owning a piece of it. But it was only ten in the morning and I didn't think Rucci would be checking up the place that early and so I took a chance. I said:

"Take him to the Rustic and meet me there. Pick a booth in the back. If you should see Rucci there, stand outside and I won't go in. Or that same cop that took us out of Crandall's last night. You get the idea, don't you, kid?"

"Why, yes," he said scornfully. "Do you think I'm a fool?"

"We won't go into that now. I don't want to meet anybody that knows me. I'm depending on you to see I don't."

"We'll be there as soon as we can."

"And bring my car with you."

"It's still at Crandall's."

"Stop by and get it. I might want it."

"As soon as I can, Shean."

I went out the side way and eased over toward the Rustic. I went damned carefully, too. Looking for policemen that knew me, as well as any of the thugs I'd met at Rucci's Three C Club. And, so help me, I just passed a hole in the wall restaurant when somebody called:

"Oh Shean! Shean, honey!"

It was the Spanish effect. Wearing slacks and a sweater arrangement and looking like a cross between a school girl and original sin.

She was nothing I wanted to see. I dragged her into the doorway of a building and said: "Now look, doll! I'm in a hell of a hurry. Something important. I'll give you a ring this evening sometime."

She pouted and said, in her funny voice: "Now Shean! Let her wait. It's a swell day and let's go for a ride. Or up to my apartment and have a drink."

"I haven't got the time, hon. Besides, it's too early to drink."

"It's never too early for me."

"You keep that idea and you'll look ten years older in three, babe. I'll call you this evening."

She said: "Are you still in trouble?"

"What makes you think I'm in trouble?"

"Well, I know Rucci. He asked me if I'd seen you. He acted anxious about it."

"Hell! It's just that maybe he wants me to go back to work or something like that."

She said earnestly: "Now listen, Shean! I'm here divorcing my husband because if I'd lived with him one day longer I'd have killed him or he'd have killed me. I'm no kid; I've been around. I know when trouble's coming. Now Rucci means trouble for you. And I heard about that shooting; those things get around. I don't know whether he was back of that or not, but he might have been. I like you, Shean, I don't want you to get hurt."

"I won't kid! It's just imagination on your part. Now I've got to go."

"You'll call me tonight."

"I said I would, didn't I?"

"Where are you staying, Shean?"

"I'll maybe tell you tonight, hon. I have to go now."

"I'm worried, Shean."

So was I, but I didn't like to admit it. I told her again that I'd call her and kept on toward the Rustic. I didn't think she'd tell Rucci anything about seeing me but there was that possibility. And even if she didn't talk she was an added complication and I didn't need anything more on my mind right then. I had plenty as it was.

I could see the front of the Rustic for two blocks before I got to it and I saw Joey drive up in his own car and go inside. Even at a distance like that there was no mistaking that big solid body and the way he carried himself. He strutted and swaggered and acted like an over-grown bantam rooster that was carrying too much

weight around the middle. I waited until I saw Lester drive up in
my car and go inside, then waited a while longer to be sure he
hadn't been followed and to give him a chance to go outside and
warn me if anyone I shouldn't see was inside.

He stayed in and I drifted up to the place and in. There was a
young fellow back of the bar that I couldn't remember seeing before
and two customers that looked as though they hadn't been home
the night before. They were up to the bar arguing with the
bartender about whether they'd been in the place the night before
and he was telling them, patiently, that he hadn't the least idea;
that he hadn't been on duty. He sounded as though he didn't care,
one way or the other. I went on past and he gave me an incurious
look and just nodded. Joey and Lester were in the back booth and
I sat down and Joey said:

"Jeese, Shean, I'm sorry you got in trouble over this case. I
wouldn't have dragged Wendel in to see you if I'd thought anything
about it. I'm sorry, kid."

"I can always quit it. Forget it. Can you dig up some dough,
quick?"

He shot a quick look at Lester, who got red in the face and
who said, very stiffly: "I gave Shean that money."

I said: "I got it, Joey. This isn't for me; it's for Wendel. For bail.
I may want to get him out in a hell of a hurry and it would take
time for him to get it from New York. He's in jail, and it's always
hard to get money when you're in the gow."

Joey laughed then. He said: "So old Tod's in the sneezer again.
Almighty Christ! I'll bet he thinks these Reno cops have nothing to
do but follow him around and throw him in the can. What did he
do?"

"Talked with his wife."

He whistled. "Did he get things fixed up at all?"

"He got thrown in jail, is all. I may want to get him out any
time. Can you get the dough?"

"How much?"

"Probably five hundred for a peace bond. But it may be that
Crandall will charge him with burglary and then the bail will run
up. Can you get it?"

He said: "I've got it here. It's his money. I wanted to explain
that to you, Shean. I went over in my account when I was drinking
and I didn't want to sacrifice anything that I was holding. I wanted
to wait until I had my regular money due. I didn't realize I'd run
over the account when I gave you that check."

"Forget it."

"Old Tod got some money from the East and I'm using it until my money comes in. I feel bad about that. I'll go down and get him out now."

"Let it go for now. I know where I can find him and if you get him out I won't."

"Well, I'll go down and find out about it, anyway." He laughed again. "I understand they don't have much use for you down around the station."

"Not one hell of a lot."

"Maybe I can fix that, too."

"How can you? The last time you were here they ran you out."

He grinned and said: "And that last time Tod and I were here we were broke. Flat. This is a money town, Shean. I've got money in my pocket now and I've found that you're treated a bit different when you have. I'll see if I can fix it."

"Try if you like."

"No harm in it. Where you staying?"

I remembered about MacIntosh not wanting me to tell where I was staying and stalled. I would have even if he hadn't spoken of it. Joey drank too much to be trusted with that kind of information. I said: "Oh I duck around. I can't stay any one place because I'm afraid of the cops getting jerry to it. So I just keep moving."

He laughed and said: "Hey, we haven't had a drink. That keeping moving is all right if you can hold up under it." He called the bar man and said to me:

"What are you drinking?"

I said: "Rye straight."

The man came over and Joey said: "Scotch for me. Hell, Connell, I thought you always took Scotch."

Lester said he didn't want anything and I said I still wanted rye. The bird went back to the bar and I said: "I'm running along after this drink. I don't like being out on the Street much. I'll get in touch with you, Joey."

"Can I depend on that?"

"You certainly can."

The man brought us the drinks and I took mine down in a hurry and stood up to go. Joey looked disappointed and said: "Hell, I can't see any reason you can't stick around and tell me all that's happened. After all, we're in the back here and nobody would see you."

"I don't like to take the chance. You got the car keys, Lester?"

Lester gave me my car keys. I said to Joey: "I'm going past Lester's hotel and I'll drop him there, if you want to stay here and lush. Or if you want to go and find out if they've got Wendel's bail set. Or he can stay with you."

Joey said: "I'm going to the station right now," and stood up with me. We all went out together and Lester and I went to my car while Joey turned up toward the station. Lester said:

"When I told him I was going to pick up your car he said he'd drive his own and meet us here. He got here before I did."

"I know it."

I started the car and got going down the street. I dropped Lester at his hotel, then went to the Palace. Half an hour later the landlady came up and said:

"Somebody on the phone for you. You in?"

"Sure," I said, and went out to the phone.

It was Kirby. He said: "I'm glad I caught you. Joey Free, this friend of Wendel's, is here and he wants Wendel out on bail. I told him bail wasn't set yet and he's throwing his weight around and demanding action plenty. I told him I wasn't sure just what Wendel was going to be charged with and he's demanding that I find out. That if he isn't charged for me to turn him loose. What am I supposed to do?"

"Joey's got it mixed, Chief. I just wanted him to find out what the bail would be and have it ready. That's all,"

Kirby said: "Okey. I'll stall him. I don't know myself what it'll be; it depends on Crandall."

"Haven't you heard from him?"

"He phoned me he'd be down shortly. That's all."

I said: "When he comes let him talk to Wendel. But you go to Wendel now and tell him not to have anything to say. About last night or anything. Get it? Tell him I said it's very important that he don't talk."

Kirby said he understood and hung up.

I went back in the room and by and by the landlady knocked again. She came in, said: "Just in case you don't know it you're spotted here. First I thought I wouldn't tell you. It's no never mind to me. But you're a friend of Mac's so I'm talking."

"How d'ya know?"

"Right after you came in I saw a car pass by slow. Like the guy was looking the place over. Now there's a guy hanging around across the street and he's been there for fifteen minutes. They've got the place staked just as sure as God makes little green apples."

"Who's the guy across the street?"

"I don't know him. A big long rangy bird." MacIntosh and Kirby were on my side and I knew the stake wouldn't be from them. Kirby would be saved trouble if I left town and MacIntosh knew I wasn't going until I had my business finished, one way or the other. That left Crandall, if the landlady was right. And I hadn't forgotten Joey Free slipping out my name there in the Rustic bar. If the bar man had caught it, and knew his boss was looking for me, he might just possibly have put somebody on my tail. But then, I'd left so soon after that I couldn't see where he'd had the time, if and providing he knew the score and had been quick enough on the trigger to catch the name. So I said:

"I'll watch it but I think you're wrong. It's for somebody else or it maybe isn't a stake."

She said: "Mister, I've run too many spots not to know a stake-out when it's put on my place. That's what it is; I'm telling you."

I said: "Thanks."

"You ought to thank MacIntosh. That's why I'm telling you."

"He's quite a guy."

"You know what he's after?"

"No."

She gave me a sharp look, started to say something and then stopped. Then she asked: "You a Sam?"

"No. Private cop. Didn't MacIntosh tell you?"

"He don't tell me things. He don't have to, most of the time. I find 'em out from other people."

"I'm after nothing that will bother this place."

"Mac wouldn't have sent you here if you were. I run a straight place. I don't care a damn how much company a man has or a girl has. I don't care if the girl is hustling or if the guy has the girl on a spot hustling for him. Get me right. That's their business. If a girl is fool enough to work for a man it's her hard luck. But I don't go for what Mac's working on.

I asked: "What's that?" without much hope of getting an answer. She snapped back: "Dope and girls together. Half the guys that have got a girl in this town have put 'em on the dope. He's on that. I don't go for that."

"I don't blame you," I said, and wondered why she was so bitter about that one particular nasty phase of the girl racket. It was a surprise; I didn't think there was much she couldn't stomach. She was that smart and hard about it. She said, and her voice sounded funny:

"I had a girl myself. Sixteen. I was living down the state then. I had her in school, in Sacramento, and sent her dough there. I didn't want her to know what I was doing, if you get it."

I said I got it.

"Well, she got tied up with a guy. A pimp and a dope head. He put her to work after he put her on the junk. Now d'ya start to understand?"

I'm beginning to."

"He brought her to the same town Mac was Marshal in. The guy stuck her with a knife and Mac killed him. He resisted arrest, according to Mac. Mac's working special on this now. I'm for him on it."

"I don't blame you."

She started to turn away, got as far as the door and stopped. She said, over her shoulder: "I don't spill my guts like this often. It ... it just happens today is her birthday. It's kind of got me down."

"Where is she now?"

She turned around then. "She's back in Sacramento with another dope-head. Still working. She's twenty-four now. Today. I ... I can't do anything about it; if she hasn't got that man she'll have one as bad. I ... I ..."

She whirled and went out of the room and I could hear her running down the hall toward her own room. I began to see plenty of reason why MacIntosh and Kirby were playing along with me. It began to tie together a bit more. Gino Kucci was in the picture a bit more, for one thing. He was the high-riding pimp type. Crandall could be either the lawyer for the bunch that was handling dope and girls or he could be the deal proper. MacIntosh would be a Government man, probably working some lone-wolf angle and not getting definite evidence that would tie in the big boys. Kirby could be after the same thing; I knew he didn't mind a rough town but that he wanted a clean town. The business I was on might tie in with the other and give them something that would stand in court.

It was an explanation that would fit, but it didn't make allowance for the dead French girl in any way, shape, or form. It did offer a possible explanation for the shooting at me angle. The operators might have some notion I was on that; coming from the City and all. I went back to the room and thought it over, right from the start.

And decided none of it held together... and that none of it would until the French girl's murder was explained.

Lester called me about three that afternoon. He said: "I'm at the hotel. Joey Free just was here. He wants to see you. He said Wendel was held under a thousand dollar peace bond and that he put it up. There were no charges filed against you or Wendel and Joey says that he doesn't think there will be any. I've just talked with him."

"Where is he now?"

"In his room, with Wendel."

"Now listen, Lester. Go down there and hold him there. Wendel, I mean. Don't let him go out with Joey. Not if you have to hit him on the head with something."

Lester said: "Gee, I don't want to do that."

"My Lord! Don't take things the way I say 'em. I mean keep him there for sure. Now hurry."

"And then what, Shean."

"Call me back as soon as anything happens."

I hung up and clicked the receiver until I got the operator. I gave her the station house number, asked for Kirby, and got him. And then said:

"Is MacIntosh there?"

He said: "Yeah! Who's talking?"

"Connell."

"He's right here."

MacIntosh drawled into the phone: "Hello!" and I said: "Look, mister. Wendel's up at the hotel. Can you get him and hold him in jail? Can you charge him with something he can't bail out on tonight?"

"I suppose I could," he said.

"Can you do it and keep it quiet?"

This was harder. It took him longer to answer. He said: "I guess I could take him to Carson City. It's Federal there, and they could hold him for investigation and not book him in a hurry. Why?"

"Will you do it now? Right away. I'll tell you about it when you get back."

"I guess I can. It's that fast, hunh?"

"I'm afraid it might be."

He said, with the drawl gone: "Okey, fella. I'm on my way down there. D'ya want me to take his pal, too?"

"No. But if you can get Wendel by himself and pick him without his pal knowing it, it would be that much better."

"You afraid of his pal?"

I said: "Will you get going? His pal goes out and lushes and would talk. Let it go at that; just hurry."

He hung up the phone. I got the operator again, got the hotel and got my fool client, and it was a relief. I stalled him with: "This is Connell. What happened?"

He said stiffly: "Free got me out, of course. I understand you didn't want him to do this."

"I wasn't anxious about it. That's true."

"So I understand. I'll say now, Connell, I don't like the way you're handling this. I suggest we meet and talk this over. The three of us. You, Free, and myself. There's too many strange things happening here to please me."

I figured MacIntosh would be at least half way there by then. I said: "You hired me to do something and it's turned out to be something entirely different. I'm doing the best I can for you; why not work with me."

He sounded stubborn. "There's too much going on that I don't understand."

"We're even. Six-two, and even. There's too much going on that I don't understand. But it's starting to work out I can tell you that. Did Crandall talk to you?"

"For a moment. He said that he didn't blame me for my action; that it was natural for me to want to speak with my wife. That she was very upset about the entire matter but didn't want to press charges against me, though she has that right. That although you and I broke into his house, he feels the same way about it. He insisted on the peace bond as a matter of routine is all. He was very friendly."

"I was afraid of that. He didn't make any more talk about a settlement?"

"We didn't discuss that. I may say, he spoke of your actions since you've been here. He seems to think he and I could have talked the matter over and settled everything between ourselves to mutual advantage."

"What do you think?"

"I'm inclined to think the same way."

I thought MacIntosh should be in the lobby by then. I asked: "You carry any insurance?"

"Certainly."

"Made out to your wife?"

"Of course."

"She's in your will?"

"Why naturally. Connell, what are you leading for?"

I said: "You dope! I'm trying to show you the reason Crandall has turned friendly. He's decided to go whole hog or none. If you're knocked off, I won't have a client and I'd go home where I belonged. Mama would collect more dough than she would from the settlement and everybody would be ahead. Everybody but you, that is. I'd win because I'm either going nuts or going out feet first. It would give me an out, you getting killed. Crandall would be ahead and so would your wife."

"You must be crazy, Connell! Crandall wouldn't consider a thing like that. The man was very friendly, I tell you. You're talking about murder, man."

I said: "The maid was murdered, wasn't she? They can only hang you once. Though it's gas they give you in this state."

He mumbled something more about me being out of my head, then spoke clearly. "Just hold the wire. There's somebody at the door."

I waited for about five minutes. Then MacIntosh's voice said: "You, Connell?"

"Yes."

"Everything's okey. I'll see you."

I said: "You damned fool! I didn't want him to know I put you on him."

He laughed and said: "He doesn't. He put up an argument and I bopped him on the side of the face with a sap. I didn't want to do it but he went off his nut and took a pass at me. I won't take that from any man, much less a man I'm trying to help. I'll see you when I get back."

"Will you make it early? I want to go out."

He laughed again. "Naughty, naughty. You're playing with fire."

"What's that mean?"

He said: "Oh hell! We've been keeping an eye on you, sort of. Sometime I'll tell you about the Spanish girl that stuck a knife through my arm once. Remind me, will you."

He hung up and so did I. There's darn little that goes on in a town of this size that the cops can't find out about if they're interested. My Spanish wonder apparently was known. She was the type, at that. To be known.

CHAPTER SEVENTEEN

The landlady brought me dinner at seven and was over her crying spell by then. She was even a bit ashamed of it. She put the tray down and said: "Lamb chops and green peas tonight. And like it. I shouldn't have blown up the way I did this afternoon but I'd been thinking about it all day. It got me down. I'm getting old; I just can't take it." I said I was sorry and that I naturally would say nothing.

She looked at me thoughtfully and said she didn't think I would. And then, still thoughtfully: "The place is still staked, if it means anything to you. Different man, but still on the job. You that hot?"

"It isn't for me."

"Was that shooting on the street meant for you?"

"Where'd you hear that?"

She said: "I've got ears. There's talk, if you know where to listen for it."

"Now look! I'm going out tonight. For a ride. Just to get out of the room. If I thought this was for me, would I do that? I'm not worried; I don't think it's for me."

"You'd be safer staying in. That's what Mac told me when you came."

"I'd go nuts looking at four bare walls."

She shrugged and said: "It's your dice, mister man. I hope you like lamb chops and peas."

"I won't go out until after MacIntosh comes. He's coming up by and by."

"He always comes up on this date. He hasn't missed in years."

She looked at me in a funny way and all of a sudden I got an idea. I said: "Say, listen! Is he some relation of yours?"

"In a way," she said. She laughed, but it didn't sound at all funny. "I married him once. We quit it when the girl was two. I couldn't stand being married to a law man, I thought. I'd been on the other side too long, you see. It's a different life. I couldn't take it and we quit and I got the girl. Now do you see?"

"More all the time."

"Mac's helped with her, right along."

"I figured him for the kind that would."

"I didn't tell you this, either. The man he shot was named Rucci. Gino's brother. There were four of them; all in the same business. Gino and Luigi are left. He got one of them then, like I told you, and the third one happened to be killed in a liquor raid down in southern California."

"Was Mac working prohibition then?"

She nodded. "Out of the Los Angeles office. The four brothers had always worked together, sort of. Mac knew that."

I said: "MacIntosh is quite a man."

She just nodded again and left.

He came up, looking grey and grim, an hour later. He planked himself down in a chair and said: "Well, your man's in jail and it's a wonder to me you can't hear him this far. He cried like a baby about it. He claimed I couldn't do it and that was when the jailer was locking the door on him."

"It won't hurt him."

"You really think he's in danger?"

"I really do."

"What about yourself?"

"I'm keeping out of circulation pretty well."

"Maude tells me you're going out tonight."

"I'm going nuts staying inside. I'm keeping off the streets." He shook his head. "I think you're a damn fool to do it with this business coming to a head. Kirby's worried; he's afraid there's nothing going to come of it."

"There may not be. I won't start anything until I'm sure of what I'm doing. I think it'll be started for me, MacIntosh."

"This girl of yours. What d'ya know of her?"

"Not a hell of a lot. She's just company."

"She's a friend of Rucci's, Connell. If that means anything."

"It means a lot. If she's right, she won't do me any harm. If she's wrong, I may be able to use her."

"What about your friend Kewpie Martin?"

"He's okey, as far as I know. At least I thought so until he came up here with one of those yeggs I battled with out at the Three C. I didn't crack to him; I don't see how he could hurt me."

"You can watch him, anyway. Maude says the place is staked."

I laughed. "Who'd stake it? You and Kirby and my partner know I'm here. That's all. If Crandall knew it, I'd have got some action before now. I think I would, anyway. I've come in and out pretty quiet; today was the first time out in daylight, since I moved in. It's possible, of course."

He said, speaking slowly: "I'm an older man than you, Connell. I've been an officer just about all my life and I've mixed with a lot of people. I've never made a mistake when I gave the other fella credit for more brains than I thought he had. Or for a lucky break. That figuring the other guy for a chump is the worst thing you can do."

"I'm not figuring Crandall for a chump. Not ever."

"And he's with Rucci. Rucci's smart. Plenty smart."

I kept my face straight and said: "I figured him for it all the time."

He looked up at the ceiling and said: "I've been trying to get something on the bastard for the last eight years and haven't done it yet. It wants to be legal, if possible. I've been law too long to go the other route."

"Sure! But if you can stick him over this business I'm on, what's the difference? He's in jail, just the same. What's the difference what he goes up for?"

He kept looking at the ceiling. He said, very softly: "We've got gas in this state. I want to have him wait to go in that chamber and I want to see him every day while he waits. I want him up for murder. That French girl may be it. It may not be, I don't know. But I can't lose, can I?"

"I think it's working out, MacIntosh."

He stood, said: "Watch yourself. Don't trust that girl, unless you're sure. Or Martin. Hell, man, in this business you can't trust anybody. I wouldn't even trust that guy I was working for if I was you. He's such a damn fool he can't see we're trying to help him."

"He's not bright. Kewp's all right; I think I've got the answer on that business of him being here. He smokes hay and was buying."

"Of course I don't blame Wendel for trying to straighten things with his wife. A man should do that."

I didn't think about how he could take it. I said: "A lot of trouble could be saved if this family trouble was straightened out when it started."

He got white around the lips and said: "Yeah! That's right, I guess. A lot of trouble."

I saved it some with: "He wouldn't have had to come out here and she'd have been saved all this divorce trouble. Everybody would have been ahead."

He said: "Be seeing you," and went out the door. He walked with a little roll, like a punch-drunk fighter. That birthday was bothering him as much as it was the landlady, and I don't think I ever felt as sorry for a man in my life as I did for him right then.

CHAPTER EIGHTEEN

I called Spanish and told her I'd pick her up in half an hour. She said:

"That's fine. Are you bringing your friend?"

I said: "Friend?"

"Well, Hazel's friend. She's here now." I said I guessed maybe I could and called Lester and told him to meet me at the corner below his hotel. That we were going calling. He brightened up, until I told him who we were calling on and then he said, in a scared voice: "Ugh... maybe I'd better not go tonight, Shean. You know I don't drink and... well... maybe I'd better not go."

"The big gal's got you scared, hunh?"

"It ... it isn't that. But she gets drunk and what can I do with her? She keeps calling me all the time. I ... ugh ... I think I'll stay home."

"Suit yourself. She's your gal."

He said: "Wait a minute," and then: "I'll meet you. Right away?"

"Yeah!"

I could hear a bunch of noise in the room and had a notion what had happened. Joey had gone in, probably with a bunch of drunken companions, and the kid had decided one woman, even if she was as big as a small pony, was easier to handle while drunk than Joey.

Just the lesser of two evils. I picked him up at his corner and he told me I'd guessed right. He said: "You know, Shean, Hazel's a lovely girl but she drinks too much. She's really nice except for that one thing."

"Why don't you reform her?"

He said earnestly, and meaning it: "D'ya suppose I could? She told me the only reason she does it is because she's so lonesome. Because of feeling so badly over this divorce. Her husband was a brute to her." I asked: "Which one?"

"What d'ya mean?"

"Which husband? She's had a lot of them, hasn't she?"

He said: "She's had a lot of trouble in her life," and sighed, and I said: "For Christ's sake, kid. You're not taking the big wench seriously, are you?"

"We've spoken of marriage, Shean."

He tried to make this grown-up and all it did was sound silly. I laughed. He got red in the face and said: "What's funny about that? I've always thought a man who didn't marry was losing a beautiful experience."

"Look around you and prove that," I said. "He's losing a chance to pay out every crying dime he makes for alimony, you sap. Grow up, kid."

"Age doesn't make any difference if there's real love between you."

I stopped the car in front of the Spanish's house. I said: "Now look. In the first place, you're not old enough to get married. This gal is old enough to be your mother. She's practically a professional at this getting married; she's got too much experience for you. And besides that. She's too big for you; she'd grapple with you and take you two falls out of three. Why, my God, kid, you could have her, another cow, and a dozen milk bottles and start a dairy route. Now lay off."

"You shouldn't speak like that about her, Shean. She's really nice."

I said: "Oh nuts. Come on in the house."

We got out of the car and I remembered what MacIntosh had said about Spanish and who'd introduced me to her. I took my gun out and held it under my coat and said to Lester: "Keep to the side and back of me. We might be walking into a plant."

"Hunh?"

"She might be Rucci's girl. I don't know."

He handed me back what I'd given him. He said: "And you talk to me about being foolish about women. And then go ahead like this."

I knocked on Spanish's door and my face was red. She opened it and said: "Come on in," and we did.

The two girls were alone in the front room, anyway, and I made an excuse to follow Spanish out to the kitchen while she mixed drinks. Just to be sure nobody was hiding there. She had her back turned and I started to put my gun away, but I was clumsy about it and she turned and saw it slide in the clip. She made her eyes wide and said:

"You're carrying a gun, Shean."

"It's an old habit," I told her.

"I knew something was wrong."

"There's nothing wrong, babe."

"I thought about it all day. That's why I went out to the Three C this afternoon. That's where I met Hazel and Mrs. Wendel."

"That right?"

"Hazel came back with me but Mrs. Wendel waited there for her lawyer, Crandall."

"That right?"

"He came out with Rucci's brother. Just as we left."

I said: "*Oh*, oh!"

"He's very nice."

"I heard that."

"Mrs. Wendel told me about you and her husband breaking in her house last night. She doesn't have any more use for him at all. She won't even talk to him."

"I noticed that."

"I think she's foolish. He'll just fight her alimony if she treats him like that."

"Maybe so, hon."

"I heard Rucci ask her if she'd talked to him and she said 'Of course not.'"

She stopped shaking drinks then and put the shaker down. She came over to me and snuggled up and said: "I'd always talk to you, honey."

"Even if you were divorcing me?"

"Of course."

"It seems funny that she doesn't talk to him, don't it?"

She snuggled closer. "Shean, you're in trouble. Is it over that woman?"

"Sort of, hon. Her old man's a friend of mine. Get the idea?"

"I don't like her. Hazel does, though. They had a long talk before Crandall came out."

"What about?"

"I didn't hear. They were over at another booth. Probably about Mr. Crandall, don't you think?"

"Probably. Let's go back in the front room."

She pouted and said I never wanted to be alone with her. I said she was crazy and that was probably the reason I was so mad about her. She said that I never acted as though I wanted to be alone with her. I said that proved right there she was crazy, but that I hated to leave Lester alone with Hazel; that they were both just young and foolish kids and might not be responsible for what they did. She giggled and said Hazel was looking for a husband. I said that Hazel had not only been looking for a husband for the last twenty-five years but that she'd been finding them and trading them in on new models as fast as she got them. She said she wasn't that type; that she was a one man woman and that I was the man. I said: "What are you going to do with those drinks? Let 'em stand there on the shelf and melt until they're no good?"

She said: "You're afraid of me because I met you through Rucci. Isn't that it?"

"Of course not, kitten."

"I just met him casually. That's all. I'll prove I'm no friend of his. I beard him say to his brother 'Tonight's the night for that Irish bastard.'"

"That's supposed to be me, babe?"

"You're Irish, aren't you?"

I laughed.

"And what did you mean when you said *'Oh, oh'*? When I said that Rucci's brother came out with Crandall?"

"That was a slip, lamb."

She got away from me and back to the shaker. She snapped: "All right. *Don't* tell me anything. I went out there just because I thought you were in trouble with Rucci and because I thought I could maybe help you by finding out something."

"I appreciate the spirit, babe."

She put the shaker and glasses on a tray and tossed her head while she headed toward the front room. But when she got to the door she stopped and said: "You might talk to Hazel and see what you can find out. Mrs. Wendel was sore about that business of last night and she was doing a lot of talking."

"Don't ever say you don't help me, sweet."

"I tried. Shean."

I said: "Let's go in the other room."

Lester and Hazel were sitting on the davenport and Lester looked a little mussed. I figured Hazel had probably been holding him in her lap; she was big enough to do the deed comfortably. He looked relieved when he saw us and she looked about half mad. I poured her three Martinis, as fast as she could get them down, then sat down by her and said: "Did you hear about the little stunt Wendel and I pulled last night on his old lady? That was funny." To prove it I laughed.

Hazel said: "Heard it! I heard nothing else all afternoon. It's a wonder you both weren't arrested."

"We were."

"She didn't tell me that. She said she didn't even know where her husband was."

I thought of the Carson City jail but didn't say anything about it. I said: "Chances are he's around someplace. He may be keeping inside, so she doesn't have a chance to raise hell with him."

"She's the kind that would. But she's so mad at him she won't even talk to him. She told me he was mixed up with some girl here, but that she doesn't want to use that against him. He beat her up last night, too, she says." I said: "Nuts!"

"Well, if I was him I wouldn't go out to the Three C any more. Or you either. They think a lot of her out there. She's there all the time."

I said: "Probably on account of young Rucci. The one that came out with her lawyer today."

"Well, she knows him of course. She must have met him lately though; she's from New York and he's from Sacramento."

"That's probably it."

The shaker went dry and she looked at it, very wistfully. I said: "Toots and I'll got out and fill it up again."

She was reaching for Lester when Spanish and I went through the kitchen door. Spanish said: "Well, did you learn anything?"

"Sure. Of course."

"I didn't hear her say anything."

"You didn't know what to listen for, hon."

She shook her head and said: "Secrets." She was about half mad and about half worried about me and I kidded her out of both before we went back in the parlor.

Lester looked a lot more mussed than he had the time before. And a lot more worried. He kept shooting me pleading glances and, finally, when Hazel got up and lumbered away to the bathroom, he came over and whispered:

"Let's go home, Shean! She's getting tight again."

I said: "You might as well learn to take it if you're going to marry the girl. My, won't life be a wonderful thing!"

"Rub it in," he said. "Let's go."

We had the shades pulled down and I'd been watching the doors all the time. Every time Spanish or Hazel got close to one I'd sit so I could get at the gun under my coat. Just in case there was something to what Spanish had heard at the Club. I didn't think she'd have cracked about me calling her that night but there was that possibility and I didn't want to be caught and not have a chance. I said to Lester:

"You take my car and take Hazel back to the hotel. I'll go out the back way and walk to my place."

"I don't want to take her home alone, Shean. She's too drunk."

"I thought you were strong for her."

"That's just when I'm not with her."

I said: "That's the way most married men feel, you dope. This is business; I think maybe somebody's waiting for me to come out of the place here. Get it?"

He said: "Well, all right, but I hate to do it. I'm sort of afraid of her."

"You're all right as long as she don't fall on you," I told him.

He looked sad and waited for her to come back from her pilgrimage.

CHAPTER NINETEEN

I left the place two hours after Hazel and Lester had taken my car away and I went out the back way. Quietly. That is, comparatively quietly. I'd have done better if the Spanish hadn't been hanging to me and begging me to stay the rest of the night where I'd be safe. She argued that all I could lose was sleep, if I stayed, and I told her that she had something there, undoubtedly, but that I had work to do.

I got to the Palace without seeing a soul that looked like anyone I shouldn't see and I went in the side door of the place as quietly as I could. But not quietly enough to keep Maude, the landlady, from hearing me. She came out of the kitchen, with a wrapper around her, and said:

"I told you it was trouble, mister. They're up in your room waiting for you."

"How many of them?"

"Two. One of them is Billy Montez and the other guy I don't know. He's a tough baby, or I'm wrong. I watched them sneak in the place."

"Who's Billy Montez?"

"He's Mexican. He smokes the weed. He's on the junk, besides that, but not bad I hear. He's a knife man, I hear. The other one is the guy that was waiting across the street for you this afternoon."

I started up the stairs and she grabbed me by the arm and said: "Oh, no you don't. I won't have trouble in my place. I won't have the spot hotted up because you want to start something you maybe can't finish. Two to one don't make sense, mister. I tell you they're waiting for you."

"What d'ya want me to do?"

"Use your head for once. Call Mac. How can you lose? I'll get him for you."

She went to a phone she had in the kitchen and got Mac, where he stayed. She naturally knew his number. I talked to him and told him what was going on and he said he'd be right over. So I sat in the kitchen and waited for him. He came in as quietly as I had, and said to her: "Now it's all right, Maude. I'll take 'em out with no fuss or confusion and there won't be a come-back on the place." And to me: "Let's do it."

"What'll you do with 'em after you got 'em?"

"Put 'em where I put Wendel. I'll have that jail filled up, first thing I know."

I said okey and up we went. We stopped outside my door and he called out softly: "Montez! This is MacIntosh. Len MacIntosh. Come out of there quietly and with your hands in sight. Or I'll come in. You hear me?"

Nobody answered. MacIntosh said again: "This is MacIntosh. Come out or I'll come in."

We could hear whispering then. Finally a voice with an accent said: "We come out. You no shoot."

"I no shoot," MacIntosh said.

He had his gun out and I had him backed with mine. The door opened and a guy with a brown, scarred face peeked out first. He saw Mac's gun staring him in the face and squealed: "No shoot! No shoot!"

"Come on out. You and your partner."

The Mex came out, followed by a man that stood at least three inches over six feet. And who didn't weigh over a hundred and twenty pounds. Just skin and bone. Mac looked him over and said: "Hagh! Boney Seitz, hunh?"

The thin man said: "Yes!" very sullenly.

We fanned them for guns and knives and didn't find a thing on either of them. I went in the room and looked around and found a Marble hunting knife under the mattress. Then an old .38 Smith and Wesson way back on the top closet shelf. And a pocket knife with a blade at least five inches long between the sheets. The knife was the kind that has a spring to snap the blade out when a release button is pressed. I said:

"Here's their hardware. There's maybe more scattered around the place but this is enough. Neither of them have a permit to carry concealed weapons, I'm willing to bet."

Seitz snarled: "You didn't find 'em on us, did you?"

MacIntosh said, very softly: "That'll be all right. By the time I'm through with you boys, you're going to be glad to claim them. Now get down them stairs and don't give me an argument. You coming, Connell?"

"Sure."

"You don't need to."

We got them outside and to his car. He had a sedan, with a coat rail on the back of the front seat, and he cuffed them together so the coat rail had the cuffs over it. Montez's right hand was below the rail and Seitz's left was over it. He said then, to me: "Go on back and get some sleep. I can take 'em over alone, as well as not."

"With the two of them in the back seat? Hell, man, I'll go with you, of course."

He grinned wickedly and said: "I don't need you. Do I, boys?"

Montez said: "You no shoot. I do nothing."

Seitz said nothing. MacIntosh waited a moment, then asked: "What about you, Boney?"

"I'm not starting anything," Boney said. "I can get bailed two hours after I'm in. Why should I start something?"

MacIntosh climbed back of the wheel and I went back in the place. Maude was waiting for me and she said: "Both those boys know Mac and both of them are scared to death of him. He's got a reputation around this country."

"If anything happened to him we'd know who did it. That ought to keep them in line if nothing else does."

"They'll keep in line. God help 'em if they don't."

I said goodnight and went to bed. Between Spanish and the company waiting for me it had been a large evening and I was tired.

The thing had dropped into place and all I had to do was wait for somebody to break it. For somebody to get impatient and start the fireworks. But MacIntosh came in the next morning and, when I'd told him what I'd figured out, said: "Why wait? Why not we start it?"

"Why not let them start it? They will soon." His eyes got red and he said: "I want it to break before that bastard of a young Rucci gets out of town. He brought two girls in with him and I can stick him on a slave charge but I want to get Gino right along with him. Let's clean it up all at once."

I said: "You're the doctor, mister," and got Lester on the phone. I said: "We're going to break it tonight, kid, if we can. Now I've got Wendel where he's safe but I don't want Joey Free worrying about him and getting things screwed up. So tell Joey that Wendel's safe in the Federal can over in Carson City. That he's being held there and isn't charged. And tell him that when I have Wendel turned loose I'll have somebody stay with him all the time to make sure he's kept safe. That I'm going to get him out tomorrow. Get it all?"

"I'll tell him, Shean. Gee, I had an awful time last night. Hazel wouldn't get out of the car. She wanted to stay in the car and ride around and see the sun rise. It was terrible."

"You came to the right place for sympathy, kid. Now listen.

Tell Joey I said not to bail Wendel out. That I'll get him out tomorrow. That Joey's to leave him there today."

I winked at MacIntosh with this. MacIntosh whispered: "Better men than Free have tried to get people out of that jail. They got locks on the doors there."

Lester said: "I'll tell Joey what you said. Your girl called and wanted to know how you are. She wants you to call her."

"Quit calling her my girl, damn you."

"You were with her last night, weren't you?"

I said: "Okey, we break even on the women," and hung up. Then I called Amos Mard and said: "Now look, Mard. Don't miss on this. Your client Wendel's over in the Federal jail in Carson City. He's just held; not charged. Get over there and wait for somebody to get him out. Don't you do it, understand. Just hang around, out of sight, and wait for somebody to do it for you. I'll have it fixed for you. Get it?"

"Not exactly. What's it all about?"

"It's wheels within wheels. That sort of stuff. Now when Wendel gets loose, you stick with him every second. It's important. It'll keep the damned fool from getting himself killed."

Mard said: "I thought of that angle. Wendel's undoubtedly carrying insurance and his wife would be the beneficiary. A dead man couldn't fight a divorce action and none would be necessary. I'll stick with him. Don't you worry."

"When you get him back here, take him up to my partner's room. That is, if you're alone. Lester will get in touch with me; I don't want you to leave Wendel even long enough to phone. It's putting you in a sort of spot but I don't think this crew is ready for wholesale murder yet. I don't think they know the break is coming as soon as it is."

"I understand."

"And if Joey Free wanders in don't crack to him about it. Even if he's sober he might not stay that way."

"I understand. But it's all right to tell Wendel the situation, isn't it? Your partner knows what's going to happen, doesn't he?"

"Hell, no. I don't myself, for sure."

"You're forcing a showdown, isn't that it?"

"That's it. Just find out who gets Wendel out of jail and then stay with Wendel every second. If he doesn't want to go to the hotel call Lester there and tell him where you are. Or better, stop by for him. He can be the contact man between us. I don't want Wendel left alone for a second."

"He's in that much danger, you think?"

"I think."

He hung up and MacIntosh got the Federal jail. He told them what was going to happen and to let Wendel loose as soon as anybody tried to get him out. But not before. They said okey and he quit talking and said to me:

"They think I'm nuts. But the trouble with so damn many of the Eastern men that come out here and try to crack up a set-up is that they think the Eastern way. It don't work out against a Western proposition. That's why I get away with the things I do; I get results every now and then."

I said: "I gather that from what I hear."

Lester called a half hour later. He said: "I saw Joey and told him what you told me to tell him. He said he wouldn't try to get Wendel out. He's drunk again; said he woke up drunk."

"Did he seem worried about Wendel?"

"At first. He said he'd been looking for him."

I said: "Okey, kid! Now Mard is coming up with Wendel, sometime during the day. Stick there and wait for them. Be ready to go out, if Wendel shouldn't want to stay there but if you go out call me and tell me where you're going! Take Joey with you if you want; it makes no difference. But don't say anything to him about waiting for Mard and Wendel. That's complicated, but you understand, don't you?"

"You mean that Mard is going to get Wendel out of jail? And that I'm not to say anything to Joey about knowing it Is that it?"

"That's the general idea."

"All right, Shean! But I don't understand what you're doing. I don't know half of what's going on. I wish you'd tell me so I could be prepared."

I said: "Hell! I don't understand half of what's going on myself. I wish I knew what was going on so I could be prepared. I don't know what's going to happen. I'm just guessing myself."

He said, very confidently: "It'll come out the way you want it to, Shean. I know that."

"I wish I had your faith. Call me and tell me if anything happens. I don't want Mard to let Wendel out of his sight for a minute, so you do the telephoning. Get it?"

"I could watch Wendel while Mard telephoned."

"You do like I ask you to," I said, and hung up before he had a chance to argue it. I said to MacIntosh: "The kid fancies himself as a bodyguard. He's a nice boy but he can't see more than ten feet away from his nose. Mard has an idea what he's facing and will have his eyes open."

"Mard's a pretty good guy. Hardly the man for the job he's got."

"Hell do. He won't let Wendel wander off into trouble and that's all I'm asking of him. The kid thinks everything's going to come out okey. He's got faith."

MacIntosh said: "I think it is myself. So does Kirby."

"I've got an idea why you're playing along with me, but why is Kirby? I don't quite get that."

He said slowly: "I've known Kirb for fifteen years and worked with him, off and on, for over half of that. We're friends. He'll play it the way I ask him if he can possibly do it. I've asked him. He ... ugh ... he knows this is sort of a personal thing with me."

"I understand."

"So does Kirby. I'll ask you just one thing. If there's trouble, leave the Rucci brothers to me. Let me take care of them. You understand; Maude told me she got wordy with you."

"I understand."

"So does Kirby," he said again.

CHAPTER TWENTY

Lester called about three in the afternoon and said that he was using a booth in the lobby because Wendell and Mard were in his room. Mard had told him to tell me that Crandall had gone to Carson City and taken Wendel out of jail. And that he'd stepped out and joined them and stuck like a leech to Wendel ever since. That Crandall had said he got Wendel out of jail because he wanted to talk settlement with him, but that he'd postponed the talk on the plea that he wanted to talk it over with Wendel first. I said: "It's working. Did Crandall let Wendel talk to his wife?"

"No. Mard told me he'd asked Crandall to let them talk it over but that Crandall said she wouldn't do it. That she never wanted to speak to her husband again."

"That's fine, Lester. Is Joey with them?"

"He was for a while but he went out to the Three C Club to get a few drinks. He said he had a twenty-eight-dollar start toward a drunk and didn't want to lose his initial investment. That he would if he let what he had in him die out. I think he's crazy.""Like a fox," I said. "Keep sticking around."

That was all for that time. The next call came at nine and I was getting worried for fear it wouldn't. It was Lester, again, and he said: "Wendel wants to talk to you. Can you meet him here?"

"Where?"

"We're still at the hotel. Mard and Wendel and I. Joey phoned once but hasn't come back."

I said to MacIntosh: "The dope has made up his mind to pay off," and to Lester: "Tell him I'll be there about ten-thirty. That I can't get there before."

"I'll tell him."

"Tell him it's the finish. And for him not to take off on some screwy angle but to wait for me. And tell Mard to hold tighter than ever; it won't be for long."

"I'll tell him."

"Okey, kid."

MacIntosh called Kirby then, and said: "Mac speaking. Listen. Take either one or two men and go down to the Golden Eagle and look it over. Look for Rucci's men. Look for anybody that's hanging around and looking suspicious. And then away we go."

"Pick up anybody that looks bad? That it?" Kirby asked.

"That's it. I mean do a first class job and really case the place. Crandall will have somebody down there waiting for Wendel and Mard to come out and I want them picked up. Now don't miss. Then call us back if we're not there by the time you're through."

"What'll I do with whoever I pick up?"

"Hide 'em. Where Ziggy Hunter won't be able to get 'em out. If you can, someplace where he won't be able to talk to 'em."

"Then what?"

"Then phone me. Get action, will you?"

Kirby said he'd get action.

We went out ready for trouble but didn't find any. We hardly expected to, for that matter; we just weren't taking unnecessary chances. We got in MacIntosh's sedan and went to the hotel and got there just as Kirby was coming out.

He wasn't alone. He had two cops with him and three men besides the cops. There were no handcuffs but you could see the men were prisoners. Kirby got over to the side and said to us: "I got 'em. Two of 'em were up the hall, outside Wendell's room. The other was in the lobby and I nailed him when we came in."

"Crandall's men?" I asked.

"Rucci's. One of them used to tend bar for Rucci at the Rustic. Another used to be the bouncer at the Three C. The other just hangs around. You know what he is."

MacIntosh looked the third man over and said: "Yeah! Big May's man, if you want to call him out of name. Anything on 'em?"

"Each of 'em had a gun. The pimp had a deck in the cuff of his pants."

MacIntosh said: "He'll talk, then. Just as soon as he has to have a shot. We'll meet you at the station. Sink these birds deep, Kirb, we're going to want 'em."

Kirby grinned and said he would and that he'd wait for us. And then MacIntosh and I went upstairs.

I could hear Wendel before I got to his room. He was damned near shouting: "I don't understand this. This is ridiculous, I tell you, Mard. This is the twentieth century; not the days of the old west. This is ridiculous."

I could hear Mard's soothing mumble and then I knocked on the door. Wendel threw it open, scowled all the more when he saw me, and snapped out:

"You've got a lot to explain, Connell. I've put up with these high-handed tactics of yours long enough."

MacIntosh and I went inside and I said: "I judge that Crandall gave you a line of crap. Isn't that it?"

"He wants to talk with me about a settlement, if that's what you mean."

"Did he tell you why he got you out of jail?"

"Of course. I couldn't well talk business while I was in jail. I understand that was your doing."

"That's right. You were safe there, weren't you?"

"Mard has been telling me of this ridiculous theory of yours. I'm perfectly safe right here. Things like that don't happen in this age, Connell."

"That's why Kirby just didn't take three guys out of the hotel that were waiting for you to stick your nose out. It just didn't happen."

Mard asked: "Is that right?"

"Right."

Mard said to Wendel: "You see. I tell you when the amount of money involved is as great as in this case, nothing is impossible."

Wendel lost a lot of bluster. "Do you mean to say that three men were waiting in the hotel to murder me?"

"That's the idea."

"Can you prove that?"

"I don't know yet. I don't think I'll have to prove it."

"What d'ya mean by that statement? Connell, I demand that you give me the facts in your possession."

I said: "Oh nuts! You'd screw things up if I did. Let it work out; it will. Now I want you to go to the phone and get Crandall on the wire. Insist on one thing. An appointment for eleven-thirty tonight. Tell him you'll be ready to discuss terms of settlement at that time. Make it at his office. If he objects to that hour, tell him you're sick of the whole dirty mess and want to pay off and leave in the morning."

"I refuse to do any such thing. Eleven-thirty at night is no hour to talk business. I've lost my faith in you, Connell, I'll tell you frankly. I'll see Mr. Crandall at a reasonable hour in the morning."

MacIntosh stepped ahead of me and said: "You'll do as you're told, for once in your life, at least. You're fooling with murder and a man is trying to save your life and you're fighting him. Use your head, man. This isn't a country or a people you know. I'll tell you now that Connell knows exactly what he's doing. He wouldn't have the co-operation he's getting if he didn't."

I couldn't see his face but he must have looked very

convincing. Wendel stepped back, said: "But... but... Who are you, sir?"

MacIntosh said: "The name is MacIntosh. I work for the Government, if that means anything. I'm concerned with more than a divorce case, mister... the Government isn't paying them attention as yet."

I said to Wendel: "For Christ's sake, man, use sense. Work it our way and it will all be over. This is serious; murder always is."

"I still refuse to believe I'm in any danger."

I said: "I bet that maid your wife had thought the same thing. But it didn't keep a knife out of her neck, did it? Now will you go to the phone and make that date with Crandall? We've got things to do before then. Better make it for twelve, at that."

"He'll probably refuse to see me at that hour."

Mard said: "People don't refuse money at any hour of the day or night, Mr. Wendel. At least they don't in Reno."

Wendel went to the phone. He acted as if the whole thing was silly, and as though he didn't approve of what he was doing, but he went. He got Crandall, told him he'd like to see him at twelve, and I could hear the phone crackle when Crandall talked back at him. This made Wendel sore. He snapped back:

"Now listen. I tell you I want to talk to you at twelve tonight. I can't talk with you now; I'm busy. If you don't care to see me at twelve, say so. I can go back East and let this matter go to court, if that's what you want."

He said, in a much softer voice a minute later: "Twelve at your office then. Mr. Crandall. Yes, I'll have Mr. Mard with me. At twelve then."

He hung up the phone and turned, with his lower lip sticking out in a pout, and said, "Is that all now, gentlemen?"

MacIntosh said: "Practically all. I'll have to ask you to stay in this room with Mr. Mard until we come back for you. We'll keep that appointment with you, you know."

Wendel asked: "And what if I don't choose to do that?"

This got MacIntosh finally. He roared out: "By the Almighty God! I'll tell you what! I'll cuff you to that bed, you young whipper-snapper, and lock the door on you. I've put in too much work on this case to have it screwed up by a young fool that doesn't realize what people are trying to do for him."

Wendel said: "I'm paying Connell for what he does," but he said it in a weak voice and started backing away from MacIntosh.

MacIntosh said: "You didn't pay Connell to stand on the street and make a God-damned target of himself for a sharpshooter across the street. They don't make the kind of money that pays for things like that. He started out on a simple little divorce case and ended up in a murder. You don't pay for that, mister."

Mard said soothingly: "I'm sure Mr. Wendel will wait here with me. Won't you, Wendel?"

Wendel said: "Yes!"

MacIntosh snorted and said: "I'd hate like hell to come back and find him not here. Come on, Connell."

Lester said to me: "Can I come too?" There'd been so many hard words that I'd hardly had a chance to look at him. He was sitting over in the corner with a bright and interested look and watching MacIntosh and me through his goggles as though he'd never properly looked at us before. I looked at Mac and nodded the least bit and Mac said:

"I guess so. He can stay back, if it gets rough."

Lester almost ran to the door before either of us changed our minds. The three of us went out and MacIntosh Crumbled: "I should take lip from a guy like that. What in the hell! All he's got is a bunch of money and I got a job of work to do."

Lester asked him: "Are you really a G-man?"

Mac said: "I guess you'd call me that."

Lester looked at him as though he was getting a peek at God and said: "I've always wanted to know a G-man. I take a great interest in the laboratory course you men have the opportunity of studying. It must be very interesting."

Mac said: "Hell, kid, I've never been east of the Mississippi River. I wouldn't fool you. I'm the other sort of G-man that just works by guess and by God."

I said: "Lester, what Mr. MacIntosh is trying to say is this. He works on the special duty that his knowledge of the country and people fit him for. He's a specialist, as it were."

Lester said: "I understand," and looked disappointed. I felt sorry for the kid; finding a God was made out of common clay must have hurt him as badly as when he discovered the Santa Claus story was false.

We got in MacIntosh's sedan and went to the Station and picked up Kirby and one other cop. Kirby looked askance at Lester and I said: "He'll stay behind, out of the way, when the going gets rough."

Kirby grunted and Lester looked hurt. MacIntosh grinned and said: "It's liable to get rough right soon," and headed the car toward the cribs. I said: "Lester, you stay in the car."

MacIntosh said: "What the hell, Connell. He ain't made of sugar or salt. Don't make a baby of him."

I said: "Okey! Lester, you can come along for the ride."

Lester beamed and wiggled a bit on the seat. He looked over at MacIntosh and, from the look, I could see God was back on earth again.

Lester wanted to see fast action... even if he didn't understand it. Mac was giving it to him.

CHAPTER TWENTY-ONE

There was forty-eight of the cribs and they were set in the shape of a horseshoe. Two long lines of little attached bungalow affairs and with a dance hall at the back. To get inside the horseshoe you had to go down a sort of lane, with a high board fence enclosing it on each side, then turn' to the right. Then you passed a little police booth, where a copper was on duty all the time. I suppose in case of disturbances; drunks and the girls fighting among themselves.

The cop had a book with the girls' names, ages, weights, and full descriptions in it. And with their records, if any. The record part was supposed to be checked but that's a hard thing to do; the girls changed all the time. The whole thing was legal, with the city taking a cut on the take.

We sailed down the alley, turned by the booth, and MacIntosh stopped there and said: "Who's new, Joe?" to the young copper in the booth.

The copper ruffled the leaves in his ledger and said in a bored voice: "Two today. Jean Allen and Frances Tremaine. Both are out of Frisco. Both are kids; Jean's twenty-two and the other's a year older. They're minding their business."

"Who brought 'em here?"

The young cop widened his eyes and said: "I don't let a pimp inside the gate, Mac. You ought to know that."

"I mean to town."

He shrugged, said: "I don't know yet, haven't heard. I suppose the usual gang."

"They on the stuff?"

He grinned on that one and said: "I'd bet a fin. I'll win nine out of ten times, won't I?"

We went down the line at the right, with the gals leaning out the windows and talking to us. They were very frank about what they were talking about; too frank for Lester. He was red in the face and so embarrassed he could hardly keep up with us. Half way down the line the cop jerked his thumb at a tall blonde leaning out of her crib and said:

"This one's Jean. Frances is at the end."

Kirby said to MacIntosh: "I'll get Frances. Get her dressed.

This is all taking time." He kept on with the young cop and Mac said to Jean:

"Okey, kid. Get your clothes on and make it snappy." She said: "What's the matter? Christ, I just got in town." He said: "I didn't ask you about that. I said 'get your clothes on.' I'm in a hurry."

She saw he wasn't fooling and ducked back into her cubbyhole. She called back: "Just a minute, Chief. You ain't getting any cherry; I been pinched before." Mac said: "Smart kid."

Lester said, in an awed voice: "Why she's hardly more than a child."

I said: "She's been farther under the barn after eggs than you've ever been away from home, kid. That's a tough baby."

"But she looks so ... well, sort of innocent." MacIntosh turned a perfectly blank face toward me and it meant more than if he'd winked. I said: "That's the kind that make the dough. *Oh*, oh! What's the Chief run into?" Kirby had stopped down toward the end of the line and there was a knot of girls around him. They weren't making any noise, though, just a sort of murmur. Through it there was a muffled screaming that cut like a knife, even though it wasn't loud. I said to the cop that had driven down with us: "Stay here and watch this gal. We want her," and followed MacIntosh and Lester to the knot of girls.

Kirby was right in the middle of it. He was on his knees, holding his arm around a girl's shoulders, and he was red in the face and swearing. He said, as I came up: "Damn that doctor! If this girl has a bad pump I'll crucify him. One of you get some water, quick. And a drink of whiskey."

One of the girls turned and headed toward the dance hall, where there was a bar. The Chief looked up at us and said:

"I told her to get her duds on and come along and damned if she didn't fold up. If she's got a bad heart I'll crucify that doctor, so help me I will."

Lester said: "Doctor!" to me. His face was pale instead of red and he kept looking around him as though he'd like to be any place but there. I said: "Sure. They look 'em over before they let 'em work. It's the law."

He said: "My God!"

I was looking at the girl. She was a good looking kid but hard looking. The blonde, Jean, had a baby face and innocent look. This kid was dark and looked tougher than tripe. But pretty. The girl came back with water and half a bottle of whisky and the bar man came with her and said:

"Let me! I know how."

He knelt down and lipped a towel in the water and started to slap the girl across the face with it. After a bit of this she started to moan and he dumped some whisky in the palm of his hand and held it over her nose and mouth. She started to strangle and cough and he grinned at the Chief and said:

"That's the stuff to give the troops. What did she do; roll some guy?"

The girl came out of it all the way then. She looked up at the Chief and sobbed out: "Oh don't arrest me. Please, please, don't arrest me. Please, please."

Lester started to look sick.

The girl went on with: "They'll put my name in the paper and my folks will find it out. Please, please."

I said to Lester: "The primrose path, kid. How d'ya like it?"

He didn't answer. I don't think he could have spoken a word if his life had depended on it. The Chief said:

"Now look, honey! I'm not going to arrest you."

And then looked up and snapped at the ring of staring girls: "Take her in and get her dressed and do it fast. Move now."

They helped her in the bungalow, and the Chief stuck his lower lip out like a bull dog and said: "She's got a lot of business here, by God. Somebody's going to answer for this."

MacIntosh said: "That's the idea, Kirb. Young Rucci is going to answer for it; that's why I want these girls."

Kirby came back to what he was supposed to be doing then. The blonde girl, Jean, came strolling down toward us, in no hurry and smoking a cigarette. The cop that had driven down with us was following her. Kirby said to the younger one, that had been in the booth:

"See that this Frances girl is dressed and okey. Glen, here will take her and Jean, here, up to the station. You understand, Glen. Just put 'em in my office and sit there with 'em. No charges and nothing to the papers. If there's a leak on this from the station I'll blame you for it. You know what to do."

Glen said: "Sure," and smiled at Jean. He was a stocky red-faced bird that looked as though he had a wife and family waiting at home. He said to Jean:

"You see? You're not even going to see our jail, honey."

She said: "It won't be the first I've seen, buttons. Or maybe the last."

MacIntosh said: "Come on, let's go," and Kirby and Lester and I started for the front. MacIntosh said to me:

"I hate to see the kids in it, like this Frances. The blonde is hard-boiled but the other just is a damned fool. This caper will hold young Rucci for some little time."

Lester said nothing and Kirby kept grumbling about the doctor not giving the girl a looking over before passing her on the job.

I said nothing either; it was none of my affair how Reno ran itself. My business was coming to a head and that's all I was concerned with at that time.

It looked as though it might be plenty for three men and a boy to handle.

CHAPTER TWENTY-TWO

The Three C Club was jammed solid when we got there. There was a car parked just before we got to it and MacIntosh slowed, then stopped by it. He said:

"We'll go in first. The three of us. But we're liable to have trouble and need help. It's here."

This was a new one on me and I said so. Kirby hadn't expected this and mentioned the fact. Lester didn't have the faintest idea of what was going on and so said nothing. MacIntosh climbed out and said: "We might as well walk in from here. One of the boys will drive my car to the front. I want to go in the back way while you and Connell go in the front."

"Who are the boys?" I asked.

I could see MacIntosh's grin in the car lights. "I'm a deputy-sheriff, ain't I? I just deputized a few of my friends. I've got that right. We're maybe going to need 'em. If we take any prisoners we'll have to have some help in getting them back."

I looked at my watch and saw it was eleven twenty. I said: "We've got forty minutes left, is all."

"That'll be plenty. Heinie, drive my car to the front for me, will you? You boys know what you're supposed to do."

A little short bald-headed man climbed from the parked car and said: "Sure, Len! We'll be watching." He got in our car and Lester said: "Shean, what will I do?"

MacIntosh answered for me. He said: "You'll stay in the car, son. This is going to be no place for you." And aside, to me: "I hope it won't be anyway. You and Kirb go in the front way. He knows who to look for and you must have an idea."

I said I had. He moved toward the back of the place, hauling out an old single-action .45, and Kirby and I gave him a couple of minutes to get around to the back and then went in the front.

We must have looked like business because Gino Rucci saw us and started toward the back. Kirby gave one look at the crowd at the bar and started to call out names. He said: "You Bates! You Wilson! Sangini! Ellis! Get back from that bar and along the wall. Jump now."

He didn't have a gun in sight but the four men moved away from the bar and against the wall. I said:

"You got it under control. I'm going back."

He nodded and said, without looking away from the four he'd picked: "Okey, go head."

I followed Rucci into the back room. He was almost at the back door when I saw him, and I stepped to one side, so my back would be against the wall, and cleared the gun from under my coat. Just in case. Rucci opened the back door, looking over his shoulder at me, and started out. He ran into MacIntosh, who was standing there. MacIntosh just reached a hand out and shoved, and Rucci, who still had his head craned back over his shoulder, twisted and fell on the dance floor. MacIntosh said: "And now?"

I just happened to turn my head toward the booth at my right, one that was facing the back door, and I saw a dark, ugly-looking monkey come out with a gun. He held it just under the edge of the table, where MacIntosh couldn't possibly have seen it, but in plain sight from where I was. He was with a red-headed girl and I could hear him growl:

"Beat it, kid! It's a sneeze I think."

The red head got out of the booth in a hurry and went past me and out in the front and I watched the dark man until I saw he wasn't going to start anything but was just waiting.

And then I looked toward the door again.

Rucci had twisted around until he was on his knees and one hand. He was only about ten feet from MacIntosh and he had to bend his fat neck up to see him. He was just braced there, staring up, but one hand was fumbling back of him.

MacIntosh maybe couldn't see the hand but he knew what it was doing. He just stood there waiting, one hand propped against the door casing and the other out of sight. All he wanted was for Rucci to make one move and it looked as though Rucci was going to make it.

Rucci was in no hurry, though. He kept staring up at MacIntosh, fumbling underneath the back of his coat. I looked at the bird at my right and saw he was half standing but that the gun was still below the table. He knew what was coming as well as I did, but he wasn't quite sure what to do about it.

I looked past him then and right into the eyes of my Spanish effect. She was sitting facing me and her mouth was open and her cheeks were so pale the rouge stood out in patches on them. Mrs. Wendel was sitting alongside of her and I could see a hefty arm and shoulder on my side of the booth that could only belong to Lester's Hazel. Mrs. Wendel apparently hadn't noticed me but was staring at Rucci and MacIntosh. Hazel of course was facing away from me. But all Spanish could see was me and I took my left hand and waved her to be quiet.

Most of the company appeared to be in some doubt of what was going on but there were three men in one booth and two in another that were wise.

The three were the same type; flashy and city. The two were old timers; men around sixty. I figured the three for friends of Rucci's and decided I'd take the bird on my right first, then switch to them.

Rucci had been on the floor for maybe ten seconds but it seemed an hour. Maybe a bit longer than ten seconds, but certainly not twice that. The red-headed girl that had been in the booth at my right hadn't had time to get to the bar. I could see Rucci's hand clear his coat tails; and could see the light flash on the gun it held: and then MacIntosh said:

"Okey! Okey! It's the pay-off!"

CHAPTER TWENTY-THREE

The shot from the front of the place, where Kirby was holding forth, started the thing off, and from there on things went like a flash of lightning. It came smashing out from the front room, sounding like a big gun, and it galvanized Rucci into action. His hand flashed into MacIntosh's sight and MacIntosh shot him. All he'd been waiting for was the excuse. At the same time I saw this I jumped for the booth at my right and slammed the man there across the back of the head with my gun, just as he brought his own up over the edge of the table and in sight.

And then I twisted, so I could see what the three in the booth were doing.

It was plenty. One of them was already out of the booth with a gun in his hand. The second also had a gun but he was still sitting down and trying to get a good solid aim at MacIntosh, who was standing in the door and swinging his own gun up. The third man was having trouble; he was sitting in such a way his gun was hanging in the clip and he was dragging gun and holster and all out from under his coat.

I took all the time I needed to make sure and let go at the second man of the three. He was all I could see, at the time, but during the second it took me to get him centered right and squeeze the trigger, I heard a little gun go off three times and a damned big one crash once. The little gun sounded like a kid's cap pistol against the noise of the cannon. My own gun's recoil threw my hand up but the second man of the three was out of the picture. I was sure of it. I'd seen his shoulders lined up against the front sight just as I shot and knew he was all through. I saw the one that had managed to get out of the booth down on the floor, saw MacIntosh still standing in the doorway, and then shouted at the third man: "Drop it, you dope!"

He couldn't have dropped it if he'd tried. The damned thing was still hung in the clip. But he quit trying to get it out and lifted both hands above his head. If he'd lifted them up any faster I think his hands would have kept on going up through the ceiling. He'd have thrown them right off his wrists.

I called over to MacIntosh: "You all right?"

He called back: "See about Kirby."

I remember the two old timers about then and looked at their booth and didn't see them. Then I saw a grey head poke up from below the table and figured I'd been right in thinking they knew what was coming. I turned and started for the front room and right as I did Spanish hit me from the side and started climbing all over me and screaming:

"Shean! Shean! Are you hurt! Are you hurt!"

I said I wasn't hurt and tried to tear her loose. I couldn't, without clipping her in the chin doing it, so I started out in the front room with her draped around me like a shawl. I got through the door and got my first sight of the front room just as more action broke out. Kirby was standing right in front of the bar, with his back to it, and he had his gun out and lined on five men now, against the wall. Another was on the floor, rolling around as though he'd heard the call. One of Rucci's pretty boy bar men had a bottle in his hand and was just getting ready to smack Kirby over the head with it and Kirby was beautifully unaware of what was coming.

I might have called out but I still had my gun in my hand and used it instead. I got my left arm around Spanish and held her tight for the second it took me to get set, then shot the bar man through the knee.

He went down and around in a spin. The heavy flat nosed bullet knocked the leg out from under him and threw him around the other, making it the center of his whirl. The back bar had a lower case, with a swell display of bottled goods, and his head went crashing through one of these windows at least eight feet back from where he'd been when I shot. And he'd made two complete circles before he hit.

Kirby had swung, to see what was behind him, and I said: "It's okey back there."

Then MacIntosh's friends piled in through the front door. Five of them. The first one held a sawed-off shotgun as though he wanted to use it, and the rest of them all had guns in their fists and the same idea in their minds.

I said to Spanish, who was now a dead weight on me: "For Christ's sake, will you lay off me now? I'm not playing."

She laid off. She let go all hold of me and slid down to the floor and I let her stay there, figuring she'd be out of the line of fire if anything more broke out. I went back in the back room and saw MacIntosh still standing in the door and still holding his gun in sight. Just as I got there he called out to the room at large:

"Everybody be quiet and nobody will be hurt. This is police."

MacIntosh's five friends kept order and we went through the crowd. Fast. We got two more that Mac thought might be friendly with Rucci, and that made eight good ones altogether. The one I'd smacked across the back of the head was breathing as though he had asthma and that meant a good chance of a fractured skull. The one in the front room that Kirby had shot through the shoulder didn't warrant a full count either, any more than the bartender I'd busted through the knee. The one I'd shot in the booth had died before his head had hit the table, and MacIntosh had shot Rucci through the chin with the slug ranging out halfway down his back. Rucci had been looking up when he'd made his play but had still been crouched on hands and knees. The one that had shot three times at MacIntosh and missed all three was just as dead. Mac had shot him through the side of the neck. So I said:

"Let's call it nine and a half on the score and not figure the three stiffs. They're out of the picture."

Mac said: "That's fair. How much time have we got?"

I looked and said: "Thirty minutes."

Lester was in by that time. He said, in an awed voice: "My God! All this happened in ten minutes!"

I said: "It all happened in less than that many seconds after it started. We've just wasted the rest of the time in cleaning up."

MacIntosh said: "We've still got time," and went over to the third of the three young fellows that had been in the booth. The only one left. The kid was standing against the wall with the other prisoners, and Heinie was watching them with the riot gun and a mean look. Just wishing for one of them to make a break. Mac reached out and took a hearty cuff at the kid's face and said:

"Where's Luigi Rucci? Quick now, punk."

The kid stammered: "He's... he's with Crao... Crandall."

Mac turned and looked at me and grinned and I said: "Be right with you. Can these boys of yours keep this crowd here for another hour? We don't want this tipped."

"They can keep 'em here all night," he said, keeping the grin.

I said: "Fine," and went back to see how Spanish was making out. I'd put her back in a booth, with Hazel to look after her.

She was feeling better. She had big black eyes and she stared up at me and said: "Honey, I thought they were going to kill you. I was sc-scared."

I said: "It's all over now. You stay here until the boys let you go and then go home. I'll see you tomorrow, for sure."

"Why can't I go back with you?"

"I've still got some business."

"Please, honey."

The shooting had knocked hell out of my nerves but I hadn't realized it until that minute. I snapped back at her: "Did you hear me tell you I had business? Now stay here like I tell you. Don't give me these arguments all the time."

She said, like a little girl: "Yes, honey."

I said: "I'm sorry, babe. It's just that I'm nervous. You stay here like a good girl."

She said again: "Yes, hon'. I don't mean to be a pest."

I said to Mrs. Wendel: "But you, lady, you're coming with me."

She put her nose in the air and said: "I refuse. I will not speak to my husband under any circumstances. If you persist in annoying me I'll be forced to ask Mr. Kirby to make you stop."

"Ask him, why don't you?"

Kirby was standing about ten feet away, talking to MacIntosh. She called out: "Oh Mr. Kirby. Will you come here a moment?" He came over and she said: "This man insists on annoying me. He now wants me to go back to town with him."

Kirby swung back to MacIntosh and said over his shoulder: "Then I'd go if I was you. I don't think he feels like fooling."

MacIntosh said: "You ready, Connell. We are."

I said to Mrs. Wendel: "You're holding up the parade. Let's get going."

She stood up, came over to me, and said: "Damn you, I'm not going."

I took her by the arm and said: "Now be nice. I don't want to get rough."

She reached out for my eyes with the hand I wasn't holding and I got my head away just in time to save the left one. As it was, I could feel her nails rip down my cheek. She panted out: "You can't talk to me like that."

Then Spanish took over. She'd managed to rip off one shoe, and she went in past me like a streak of light and started nailing away at Mrs. Wendel's face with the high heel. She got home with it three times before I could catch her and before Kirby could grab Mrs. Wendel and get her away, and I said to Kirby: "Let's go, for God's sake."

Spanish, when I left, was sitting in a booth with her head down on the table and crying as though her heart was breaking.

Just a bundle of nerves. Both of us.

We got to the hotel at ten minutes of twelve and I got out and said: "I'll go up and get them."

MacIntosh said: "I've been thinking. It would make it better if he talked to Crandall without her being along.."

He jerked his head at Mrs. Wendel.

I said: "What are we going to do with her?"

He said: "Now look! Both Kirb and I know that building. Suppose he and Lester and I go up there now. We'll stake out and be handy. We'll take her with us. Then you come up with Wendel and Mard. How's that?"

I said: "It'll be swell, if you don't leave me on any spot. That's liable to be tough."

"We'll be there."

I said okey and went inside. I stuffed fresh shells in my gun, going up on the elevator, and the boy gave it a goofy glance and said:—.

"Gee, mister, that's a regular cannon, ain't it?"

I said: "Why fool around and expect a boy to do a man's work," and started down the hall toward Wendel's room.

And met him right at the door. He was coming out with his head turned back toward the room, and he was saying to Mard: "I certainly shall keep the appointment after I made it. I tell you Connell is crazy."

I stuck my finger in his ribs and said: *"BOO!"* and back he went, caroming into Mard and almost knocking him down. He was shaking so he could barely stand. I said:

"That stubbornness of yours is going to get you in trouble, Mr. Wendel. Are you ready?"

He got himself together and said he was. I said: "Okey then, let's start. We'll go in my car."

"Where... where is Mr. MacIntosh?"

"He went home and went to bed. He decided the whole thing was a fake, right from the start. That I'm crazy, just like you thought."

He said he'd known I was wrong and that he'd tried to tell me but that I wouldn't listen. Then the door across the hall opened and Joey Free came out of it and saw us and said: "Hi, Shean! What's going on?"

I said: "I'm crazy, that's all. Wendel, here, is going up and talk settlement with Crandall. After all, Crandall got him out of jail after I put him in. Maybe Crandall is really okey, after all."

Wendel said: "You have to expect him to do his best for a

client. After all, he's my wife's lawyer, not mine. He's bound to look after her interests."

I said: "You bet. Even if he has to frame you with an assault charge against a minor to blackmail you into a settlement. He's a fighter, that man."

Wendel shut up and I could see Mard's grin. Joey said:

"Should I come along? After all, I'm Tod's friend."

I said: "Sure, why not? You and Mard can go in your heap and Wendel and I will ride in mine."

"Tod and I can ride together. We'll meet you; we'll just stop at the Rustic and have one drink."

I said: "Tod's going with me, because he's late now. You follow us."

I got Wendel by the elbow and started him out the door, which stopped the argument. He told me, all the way down in the elevator, and all the time it took for us to drive to Crandall's office, just what a fool he'd been to try and fight the divorce. That if his wife didn't think enough of him even to talk k over with him he was better off without her.

The talk didn't fool either of us. He knew and I knew that he was as crazy about her as ever and that the only reason he was agreeing to a settlement was because she wanted it. I felt sorry for the poor duck ... a man in love is always a pitiful thing.

CHAPTER TWENTY-FOUR

Crandall's office was just as big and pretty as it had been before. Only this time, instead of the dignified looking young punk who'd done the honors in the front office, we met the two guards who'd raised hell with us when we'd crashed Crandall's house. The one called Barney opened the door for us and grinned at me and said:

"Yowsuh! He's waiting for you."

Wendel said: "I was slightly delayed."

I said: "There's a couple more coming in a minute. His lawyer and his friend."

"I'll send 'em in."

There was a water cooler over in the corner of the room and I took one of the paper cups that came along with the rig and took myself a drink. Wendel watched me with an impatient expression and I said:

"Okey! In we go. To beard the lion in his den."

"What!"

I said: "Read the classics. It goes something like 'And darest thou then to beard the lion in his den, the Douglas in his hall? And hopest thou hence unscathed go? No! By St. Bride of Bothwell no! Ho, Warden, ho! Let the portcullis fall, Marmion.'"

He said: "Are you crazy?"

I said: "Just educated. Scott wrote it; if anybody's crazy it was him." And to the one called Barney: "Suppose you let us in, portey."

He said: "What!" also, and I shook my head and told him: "You weren't listening. You're riding for what they gave the portcullis."

"Hunh."

I said: "A fall, dope. Show us in to the old marster."

He shook his head as though I'd been talking gibberish, which I'd been. And no mistake about it. I felt that way; the show-down was coming up in the next few minutes, one way or the other, and I felt tight and tense and like babbling.

Too much nerves.

We went inside and there was Crandall, all alone. But he said to Barney: "Suppose you stay in here, Barney. The gentleman..." he nodded at me ... "is inclined toward violence and I'm in no mood for it."

I said: "I can always wait until you *are* in the mood. I'm a patient man."

He grinned nastily and said: "I should think by this time Connell, that you'd have learned your lesson. Every time there's been trouble between us your side has lost."

I looked over at the floor by the door, where he'd fallen the time I'd smacked him, and he got red in the face. He let it go, though, and said to Wendel:

"Your wife refused to attend this little meeting, though I tried to persuade her to be present. But I hold her power of attorney, of course. I'd rather Amos Mard was here however; I understand he's representing you."

"He'll be here shortly," Wendel said.

"That's fine, that's fine."

I said: "He and Joey Free are following us."

Crandall gave me a sharp look.

Wendel said: "Now understand me, Mr. Crandall. I'm willing to sign this settlement because I believe Ruth wants this divorce. Naturally, I want to be fair with her. Your threat about that assault charge hasn't influenced me in the slightest."

Crandall said: "Of course not. I'm glad I was able to stop that. You understand, Mr. Wendel, a wealthy man is a target for schemes of different kinds at all times. Possibly this was something of that sort."

"Does that mean," I asked, "that there'll be no assault charge filed if this settlement doesn't go through?"

Crandall smiled his lawyer, smile. "Now Mr. Connell. Naturally I can't hazard an opinion on that. I wouldn't know. The girl's father could undoubtedly press the charge anytime he saw fit."

"Then Mr. Wendel is liable to take it on the chin, whether he signs this settlement or not?"

"I'd naturally use my influence to stop anything like that."

I said: "That's certainly white of you."

The other plug-ugly brought in Amos Mard and Joey Free then. Mard nodded to Crandall and Joey beamed around at one and all and said:

"Hah! Everything friendly, I see.

Crandall said to Mard: "I have everything drawn up, Amos. If you'd care to look over things? It's just a form, of course."

Mard said nothing and reached out his hand and Crandall handed him papers. He studied them for a bit, while Joey babbled about wanting to go back to the city because Reno was too rich for his blood. He stopped for breath and I said:

"It's been pretty rich for Wendel's blood, I'd say. Or don't dough like this settlement count as money."

Wendel said stiffly: "I'll ask you not to comment on my personal affairs, Connell. I feel this matter could have been handled differently from the start and I don't hesitate to say so."

Joey winked at me and said: "I guess you're sat on, old boy, old boy."

Mard looked up then and nodded at me. I said: "I come up smiling, Joey," and to Crandall: "D'ya mind if I get a drink of water? I ate something salty, I guess."

I nodded toward the outside office, where the one yegg had gone and where the water cooler was, and he said:

"Certainly not, Connell. In the other room."

Joey said to Crandall: "*You* ought to buy a drink, Crandall. Not water; I don't mean water."

Just as I got to the door Crandall said: "A very good idea, Mr. Free:"

I went outside.

The yegg was sitting in an over-stuffed chair looking at the cartoons in The Satevepost. And he didn't look as though he knew enough to read the captions, much less understand the cartoons themselves. I waved at the cooler and said: "Drink."

He nodded and I walked to the cooler. It was at his side, maybe five feet from him, and I got one of the trick paper cups and fiddled with it and he looked down at the magazine again. I took my gun out from under my coat and bopped him across the jaw with it. He just dropped his head down on the magazine without a sound. I opened the door into the hall, very quietly, didn't see anything of either Kirby or MacIntosh, and whistled. They came around the bend in the hall and up to me and I saw MacIntosh had a nice start toward a black eye and more scratches on his face than I had. I whispered: "Where's the bitch?"

He jerked his thumb over his shoulder and said: "She doesn't want to talk to her husband. She says so. She fights against it even. D'ya want her? The kid's looking after her so we can help out if it's needed."

I said: "Everything is okey in the outside office. Get ready to come in when I sing out. Bring her in with you."

He said: "All right," and I ducked back inside the inner office again. Barney looked at me suspiciously and Crandall nodded at the bottle and glasses he had set out on the table and said: "Drink, Connell?"

I said: "I just had one."

Barney said: "And it took you long enough, too."

"I was thirsty."

"You must've been."

He stood and started toward the door and Crandall said sharply: "Sit down, Barney! Everything is all right."

Barney sat down, glowering at me while he did.

Mard said, slowly and carefully: "Now again, Mr. Wendel, I'll advise you against signing any ridiculous settlement like this. I advise you to start a counter-suit and fight this."

Joey wandered over to the desk and tipped the bottle over one of the glasses. He turned with the glass in his hand and said to Wendel: "It's your affair; Tod. Naturally, I hate to see you and Ruth having trouble; I like you both. But God knows you've tried for a reconciliation and that's about all you can do."

Wendell pulled his chair over to the desk and reached out his hands for the papers Mard still held. He said: "Let's get it over with. Where do I sign?"

He sounded sick and sorry.

Crandall leaned across the desk and marked lines with a penciled cross and said: "Here, and here, and here."

I said: "I guess maybe you'd better talk with the lady first Wendel," and then called out:

"Bring her in, Mac!"

I was watching Joey Free's face and I didn't expect the look he put on. It had everything in it. Shock, surprise, bewilderment, and I'm damned if he didn't look as though he wanted to laugh on top of it all. He stood up there holding his drink and staring at the door.

I swung around and looked and I didn't blame him. It was more than I expected to see. MacIntosh was holding the door open, standing inside the room and looking mean.

Lester and the girl were in the doorway, with Lester slightly ahead. They'd made sure he'd handle her. He had a handcuff on his right wrist and he had his left hand over on the chain and he was pulling the girl into the room. She had one pair of cuffs on her wrists, holding them together, and the other side of Lester's cuffs were snapped over that chain. He was pulling on her as if she was a balky mule.

But that wasn't the payoff. She had one handkerchief tied

across her mouth and another holding her chin up so she couldn't
open it. She looked like she had the mumps. All she could do was
make whimpering noises. She hung back in the doorway, with
Lester tugging away and not doing any good by it, and then I saw
Kirby's face show up over her shoulder. Then he shoved her in the
back and she came skating into the room.

Wendel shouted: *"RUTH!"*

I said: "Take the wraps off her puss."

Crandall stood up and bawled out: "This is an outrage. Are
you trying to force this woman in here?"

Barney reached under his coat for his gun and I let him see
the one I was holding was pointing at him and said:

"I wouldn't! Or do as you like!"

He took his hand away from his coat as though he'd burned
it there.

Wendell stood up and I stood up at the same time. He started
to run toward Lester and the gal and I got him by the shoulder and
yanked him back and threw him in his chair. I said: "Stay there,
you."

Crandall said, very loudly: "You can't force this woman like
this. Mrs. Wendel, I'll take care of this."

During this time MacIntosh had reached over and ripped the
handkerchiefs away from her face. She spit out another one, that
didn't look too clean even at that distance, and tried to kick
MacIntosh in the shins. Her' eyes looked like black fire and she
was bouncing up and down like a dancing doll. Lester was trying
to hold her, but he needed more than cuffs to do it; he needed
about a hundred pounds of weight. I could see why they'd tied her
to him.

Wendel shouted: *"Ruth!"* again, and I said: "Will you shut up
and stay down? This gal is Madge Giovanatti. She isn't Ruth. Tell
him you're not Ruth, honey."

She spoke then. She said to me: "You dirty bastard!"

Crandall said: "Mrs. Wendel! I forbid you to talk."

I said to Wendel: "Are you satisfied, mister?"

He sat there with his mouth open. I said again: "You satisfied?
Her name is Madge Giovanatti. She's a San Francisco tart."

She spit out something at me in Italian and "bastard" sounded
like a pet name compared to it.

MacIntosh said: "I guess this is enough. You're under arrest,
Crandall. And you too, mister."

This last was to Barney.

Wendel said, in a dazed voice: "This... this isn't my wife."

I said: "That's what I'm telling you."

I'd been watching Joey Free. He was staring first at the girl, then at me, then at MacIntosh and Kirby. All around the room. He was still holding his glass of whisky but he had it up around the level of his chin.

Crandall said: "What am I being arrested for? If this is a fraud, I'm no party to it. Naturally not."

And then drooped his eyelid in a deliberate wink at the girl.

I said: "Well, that's only one of the charges. Fraud! There's murder, too. Attempted murder with me as the victim will be another. And Mr. MacIntosh has a few little Stags against you. White slavery and dope and little odds and ends like conspiring to defeat justice. Laugh all that off too."

Joey Free said: "Well isn't *this* something."

I said: "The same is going against you, Joey. Except the dope and slave charges."

He said: "*What!* You're crazy, Shean!"

I said: "I'm getting sick and tired of being told that I'm crazy. Now listen! The..."

Mard almost screamed: *"Look out!"* and pointed toward the door, and I started to turn my head. Joey pitched his whiskey, glass and all, into my face then. I went blind for a second and a gun crashed out, sounding like a cannon in the confined space. I didn't know who it was meant for and didn't see any reason for sitting in the chair like a turkey at a shoot. I rolled off the chair to the floor and somebody, it must have been Joey, kicked me in the face about the time I landed.

I kept on with the roll, trying to get away from another kick. I was holding my gun in my hand and the next kick caught me a glancing blow across the forearm, but I still kept it. I opened my eyes, saw dimly that Joey was following me up, and reached up and out with the gun and pulled the trigger.

He came down on top of me and it took me a second to shake him off. Not because he was trying to hold me but because he was so heavy. I got up to my knees and faced the door and saw Kirby leaning back against the wall. His shoulders were touching it but his feet were a foot and a half away and he looked as if he was trying out some acrobatic trick. MacIntosh had a gun in his hand and just as I saw it he fired. Toward Barney, I thought, though I didn't turn my head enough to be sure. The bird I'd bopped on the chin in the outside office was standing in the doorway and he shot at me just as I recognized him.

He didn't miss. Not entirely. I felt something like a hot iron being laid across the side of my neck and then shot back.

I didn't have time for any fancy stuff and I wanted to stop him quick. Just as the front sight came up to where his dark pants and light shirt made a line I pulled the trigger. He stooped way over, put both hands around his belly, took a step ahead and fell. I knew that this time he was out for good.

Lester and the girl were on the floor. She'd yanked him down there when the thing started, I found out later. I even noticed he'd lost his glasses in the scramble. I looked over at Barney and saw him leaning over the arm of his chair. He was still holding a gun but he didn't look as though he had any use for it. I kept swinging my head and didn't see Crandall and decided he was back of his desk. I kept on with the swing until I saw Joey Free, and Joey was flat on his back and dead to the world.

The room was racketing with echoes from the guns and the girl was screaming through the din. Her voice wasn't so loud but it cut through because it held such fear. She was trying to crawl to the side of the room and she was dragging Lester with her.

Kirby started to slump down to the floor then, and I got the rest of the way to my feet and started toward him. And got halfway there when another man stood in the doorway.

I'd never seen him but I would have known who he was if I'd met him on the street instead of in Crandall's office. He had Rucci written all over him. The young one, Luigi Rucci, and no mistaking him. He and I shot at the same time but I got up and he didn't. I took mine through the leg and he took his through the face. His slug didn't even touch the thigh bone and mine took the whole back of his head away with it.

Things got hazy then but I remember MacIntosh howling at me for killing that particular Rucci and not saving the guy for him and me howling back about how I wouldn't stand up and play clay pigeon for him or any other son of a bitch on earth.

We were both excited.

Kirby, whom Barney had got in the shoulder with the first shot, and I, went to the hospital in the same ambulance.

Joey Free rode by himself in another but he was always one for attention He even had a policeman with him all the time after they'd patched him up. My slug had caught him just below the knee and ranged up the whole length of his thigh. They dug it out up by his hip but they had to cut off his leg to find it The leg wasn't any good to him, anyway; that flat-nosed .45 had pulverized the bone during its trip.

Lester rode to the hospital with Kirby and MacIntosh and I rode to the jail with Crandall and the gal.

Altogether everybody took a trip, but it was a one-way ride for Barney, Barney's pal, and the young Rucci.

CHAPTER TWENTY-FIVE

Wendel came to see me about noon the next day. He sat down by the cot and said: "Joey didn't break, but Crandall did. He'll testify against Joey and save himself that way. State's evidence. The District Attorney seems satisfied so I guess it's all right.

I said: "Let me tell it. Joey, on that trip East he made a while ago, saw your wife and realized she was a dead ringer for this Madge Giovanatti whom he knew in San Francisco. He got your wife's maid in the frame, then. They got your wife out of the way and the thing was started. Right?"

He said: "Right!" in a sick way.

I said: "I hate to ask; I know how it makes you feel. What did they do with her?"

"They... they killed her there in my house. They... weighted her body with wire and iron and put her in the river. My God, how can people do things like that."

He took a cry for himself, then braced.

I said: "Joey knew he couldn't handle it by himself and he'd known one of the Ruccis in San Francisco. So he tied in with Gino, who put him in with Crandall. Crandall was the front man; that's all. Right?"

He nodded.

"That was a mistake. MacIntosh had been laying for that Rucci family for years and he was taking any angle that might help him get them. Of course Joey couldn't know that. I knew there was something wrong with Joey from the start."

"How? That's what I don't understand. How you knew Joey was back of it. Why he even introduced you to me in the first place and influenced me into hiring you."

"That was so he'd know what was going on all the time. Cinch. I'd naturally tell him how I was doing. He had Rucci and Crandall warned about me before I ever got here; Rucci gave me a job for the same reason. Just to watch me. That was self evident. And then, as soon as this Madge Giovanatti saw me with two guys that had known her in the city they got panicky and tried to kill me. Who did that shooting?"

He said mechanically: "The man you killed in the doorway. One of the two guards. Free was in town at that time, though he was supposed to be in Los Angeles, and hired the man to do that; Crandall claims he didn't know anything about it until after it had happened."

"Maybe he didn't. That was the tip-off about the girl being the ringer, though I didn't realize it at the time. What put me wise was her not talking to you. Any woman that leaves her husband will talk about it to anybody that will listen. Even to him. Hell, she'll talk to him about it quicker than anybody else."

He grinned a little faintly and said that seemed reasonable.

"And that ringer theory fitted in with the maid's death. They had to kill her because she realized what she was mixed up in and got cold feet."

"Crandall claims he didn't know anything about that, either, until it was done."

"The same man that shot at you ,did that. Crandall didn't know about it he claims."

"He would. Well, I guess that's all of it. I knew Joey was wrong all the time. He tagged me to the Palace and tried to get me knocked off there, too. He was the only one logically to suspect, the way the play came up. He was tipping Crandall and Rucci all the time and I played him for it."

"Why did you figure he was back of it in the first place?" I laughed and said: "Hell! When a guy with the money he was supposed to have, puts out a rubber check for a hundred bucks and has a time making it good, it's time to figure he's not in the dough. You were. He wasn't. He'd naturally be trying to dope out a way to screw you out of it, wouldn't he? His playing drunk all the time was just a gag; it gave him a chance to meet them and talk."

He said: "I should have realized you were trying to protect me and given you more co-operation. But I'll confess, frankly, there was a personal feeling back of that lack of cooperation. It's a hard thing to say, but you grated on me. I'm sorry about it."

"What the hell! Your life and mine have been a bit different. That's all. You did more than grate on me, mister, you damned near drove me nuts at times."

He grinned and handed me a check and said: "If it isn't satisfactory, just say so. I know you will; you're very plain spoken, I'd say."

I looked at the check and he said: "It won't come back to you, like Joey's did. I'll promise you that."

"Swell," I said. "I hope you keep your promises."

We shook hands and told each other how much we admired

each other for our good qualities and the rest of that kind of talk and he left. He was getting the two o'clock plane for the East. I felt sorry for the poor duck; he was taking his wife's murder like a man, which was more than he'd done his fake wife's divorce case.

I'll always think hurt pride had something to do with that.

Lester and Spanish came up at four; the doctor was shortening me on visitors until I got back some of the blood I'd lost. The crease on my neck had bled plenty and the slug through my leg hadn't helped. They came in and Spanish flopped on her knees by the bed and grabbed my hand and said:

"Oh Shean! Shean! I've been almost crazy since I heard about that terrible thing last night."

I said: "Nuts, lamb! I'm practically well right now."

Lester said: "Did Wendel pay you? He's left." I said:

"He paid, and how," and Lester lost his worried look and said that was fine. I told Spanish to act like a lady and sit in a chair like one and she gave me a dirty look but minded. I asked Lester:

"What's happened at the station?

"They sent that one poor girl back to her folks. The other one paid her own fare back to Sacramento. Mr. MacIntosh and a bunch of other Government men are arresting a lot of men and taking them to Carson City. On the same charges he was going to arrest Rucci for."

"White slave and dope, eh?"

He nodded, and said: "He's coming to see you tonight. You and Mr. Kirby. He said to tell you something like striking an iron while it was hot. It wasn't the old saying but something that meant it, if you know what I mean. He's very pleased; he says he's really cleaning house."

"How's Kirby?"

"I asked the doctor. Getting along fine. He fired the policeman named Hunter; Hunter was working for Crandall."

"That's swell. How's your big girl? Hazel." He put on his worried look again and said: "I'm supposed to meet her at five. How long will it be before you're able to go back to San Francisco?"

I laughed on that one. Spanish leaned over and took my hand and cooed: "Honey! If I go to San Francisco to live, after I get cured, will you come and see me?"

She was talking her gargly way, as usual, and I looked at her and thought how pretty she was and how I didn't like her voice one good damn's worth, and I suddenly thought of something and got curious. I doubt that I would have had nerve enough to come out with it if I hadn't been a bit lightheaded from losing blood. I asked:

"Listen, doll! Do you, by any chance, happen to be wearing a dental plate?"

She looked startled as well as red in the face, and stammered: "W-w-well, yes. It's partial."

"I'll buy you one that fits as soon as we get to the city. I made dough enough out of the case to afford it."

Lester said, in a shocked voice: "Shean! You shouldn't say things like that."

"If she isn't used to the way I talk by now, she soon will be. Won't you, lamb baby?"

She grinned at both of us and said: "I *love* it. I never know what's coming next."

Lightning Source UK Ltd.
Milton Keynes UK
UKHW041457090223
416564UK00011B/186

9 781515 426240